Laurence William Maxwell Lockhart

Fair to See

Vol. III

Laurence William Maxwell Lockhart

Fair to See
Vol. III

ISBN/EAN: 9783337051655

Printed in Europe, USA, Canada, Australia, Japan

Cover: Foto ©Andreas Hilbeck / pixelio.de

More available books at **www.hansebooks.com**

FAIR TO SEE

A NOVEL

BY

LAURENCE W. M. LOCKHART

AUTHOR OF 'DOUBLES AND QUITS'

IN THREE VOLUMES

VOL. III.

WILLIAM BLACKWOOD AND SONS
EDINBURGH AND LONDON
MDCCCLXXI

FAIR TO SEE.

CHAPTER XXVII.

AFTER parting with Eila, Bertrand Cameron wandered about the streets for hours in a purposeless sort of way. He had nothing to do —no object whatsoever—till to-morrow morning, when, at all events, he should see Eila again, and when he hoped she would be so far recovered as to admit of the discussion of their plans. He had nothing to do but think; and so he walked about, pondering in deep trouble on all their griefs and perplexities.

Her agitation had been most distressing, and it was all on his account; her illness most alarming, and he was the cause. What fathomless depths of love and generosity there were in a woman's heart! How she would have sacrificed herself for him!—even traduced herself to his uncle to save his fortunes, and accepted the lot of a lonely and loveless life that it might be well with him! Well with him! How little she could have comprehended the depth of his love! |But it showed how noble was her nature. Her resolution to persevere in this absurd self-sacrifice would, of course, give way before his calm expostulation. She was agitated and hysterical when she spoke of it as unalterable. Of course it would give way. She was certain, however, that her father would never consent to their marriage under the circumstances. Be it so. At all events that would remove the painful feeling that he gained anything in marrying her but her own beloved self. It might be looked upon as a sacrifice for her to make; but, judging by his own experience, that would only enhance her pleasure in bestowing herself upon him, even in opposition to her father. There was quite a singular harmony in the way things were running—such coincidences —such unparalleled love—such probable mutual sacrifices. Everything cast to the winds by both —friends, fortune, prospects—everything—all for love! It would be a sight for the gods if Mr M'Killop *did* refuse his consent, and he and Eila

went forth to face the world in a state of beati-
fied beggarhood. Then there would be an end
of a disgraceful connection for her and for himself; and if it entailed poverty — even abject
poverty—that would be better for them than
wealth coming through a channel which made
the purity of its origin doubtful. As a result of
his cogitations, he came to the conclusion that,
notwithstanding Eila's wish to the contrary, he
had better see her father at once. No good
purpose, he assured himself, could be served by
postponing the discovery of Mr M'Killop's actual
views. Time was precious; and if an elopement
had to be resorted to, he might as well employ
this evening in maturing the plan for it. Besides,
Mr M'Killop would think it strange if he was not
informed that day of Sir Roland's decision. Mr
M'Killop had a right to expect the earliest information from him; though how, if that gentleman
pressed him for Sir Roland's real reason for absolutely forbidding the marriage, he was to get
out of the difficulty, he didn't quite see.

But, after all, if M'Killop was guilty—of which
Bertrand was not sanguine enough to entertain
a doubt—he would certainly conclude that his
own crime and Sir Roland's veto were cause and

effect, and say nothing about it ; whereas, if by
chance he was innocent, he had perhaps the right
to have an opportunity of vindicating himself.
That was a consideration, and a grave one. On
.the whole, he would call upon him, and be guided
·by circumstances ; and so he turned once more
in the direction of the hotel.

It was not a pleasant interview to approach.
Apart from the communication he had to make,
which was bad enough, he had to combat the
loathing he felt for this man—this man with the
taint of felony and the shadow of the jail upon
him—this man, whom, under ordinary circumstances, he would have shunned as if plague-
.stricken,—it was not a pleasant thing to go to such
.a person and ask him if it was still his pleasure
that they should become relatives. But then,
·Eila——; it was only another sacrifice made for
her, and that was sufficient.

With these feelings, he was ushered into Mr
M‘Killop's presence. Our fates and fortunes, as
every one has remarked, seem constantly to hinge
upon some trifling little condition ; and the future
events recorded in this history were very materially affected by the circumstance that, when Bertrand made his visit, Eila was, to his disgust, not

visible—that, indeed, she was unconscious of his presence in the house, and was at the time engaged, not in invaliding on the drawing-room sofa, as he had expected, but very earnestly in the composition of a letter in an upper chamber. If, when she had finished and despatched her letter, she had come down-stairs at once and seen him, even then the course of events might have been entirely changed; but she didn't, and so—why, so they weren't.

M'Killop rose to receive Bertrand with smiles of welcome. He said he was delighted to see him—and so no doubt he was. For these long weeks that had been so dreary for the young lover, had been passed by his intended father-in-law in anxiety and impatience. Mrs M'Killop said that he had actually displayed more impatience than he had done during the three weeks intervening between his betrothal and marriage to her; and although we may doubt the severity of this test, the admission proved that M'Killop's state had been far from that of his normal quiescence.

"Come at last, Bertrand," he cried, holding out both his hands. "My daughter has left all the good news to be told by you; I've not even seen her to-day. But to show you how impatient

I have been to congratulate you (for the moment
I knew you had come in person I knew that it
was a case for congratulation), I have been five
or six times at your hotel already this morning;
I suppose you have been with Eila. Well, well,
it was only natural; but now sit down and let
us hear all about it. I thought you were to
telegraph ; but, after all, it is pleasanter to learn
things by word of mouth."

Although M'Killop spoke with all this confidence in the goodness of the news, there was a
perceptible nervousness in his manner, and a sort
of questioning look in his eyes, as Bertrand seated
himself—in silence.

" Well," said M'Killop, as the silence was not
broken—" well? what says his Excellency ? "

" His Excellency's letter is not a pleasant one,
Mr M'Killop," said Bertrand, in a grave, sorrow-
ful tone, with his eyes fixed on the ground.
M'Killop caught his breath as if touched by a
sudden spasm ; something seemed to vibrate all
through him, and every line of his face was
changed as if by the effect of galvanism.

These symptoms were lost upon Bertrand, till,
after two or three ineffectual efforts, during which
he seemed to be labouring for breath, Mr M'Kil-

lop spoke: then so altered, strange, and discordant was the sound of his voice, that Bertrand started and looked up, and, seeing the miserable change which had come over the man's appearance, felt that his guilt was beyond a question.

" His Excellency's letter is not so pleasant as we had hoped?" said M'Killop, slowly, as if trying to collect his composure.

" Much the reverse, I am sorry to say," replied Bertrand, again looking down.

" He thinks, perhaps, that this engagement has been entered upon too hurriedly?"

" He does not dwell specially upon that."

A pause, during which Bertrand was trying to decide whether it was his duty to disclose unreservedly the contents of his uncle's letter.

" Not specially upon that?" repeated M'Killop, mechanically; and then, " I am to understand that he withholds his sanction?"

" Yes."

" Unconditionally?"

" Quite; absolutely."

" Gentlemen at his time of life have their crotchets" (M'Killop went on talking pretty much at random); "object to early marriages, and so forth. He is jealous, perhaps — men in his position are apt to become exacting — of not having been consulted before the engagement was made?"

"He *does* say I was bound to consult him first of all."

"Oh," said M'Killop, with a slight gleam of hope, "we must humour him a little; we must talk him over—we mustn't despair: perhaps he won't say 'No' a second time."

"Indeed he would, if I ever asked him again, —which I certainly am not going to do."

"No? He has forbidden the subject?"

"Nothing more will pass between us, Mr M'Killop, on that or any other subject; all connection is broken off between us."

"Good heavens, Bertrand! what is this?"

"Simply, that he has forbidden the marriage on pain of my disinheritance, and I have declared for disinheritance."

M'Killop, who had risen, fairly staggered back into his chair at these words, and sat for some time, rigid and motionless, staring at Bertrand without a word. At last he started up, and cried out with great vehemence—

"This is madness! sheer madness! it must not be—it shall not be; you shall not ruin your-

self; I will not suffer it. God forbid that I, or
daughter of mine, should bring this upon you.
Give up the marriage, give up everything, rather
than lose your uncle's favour: you can get a
hundred wives, but you have only one birthright.
Write to Sir Roland—write, and say that you
bow to his wishes."

Bertrand was both surprised and touched by
M'Killop's disinterested regard for his welfare.
It appeared to him that this man, who had been
guilty, was magnanimously unwilling that the
consequences of his guilt—long past, and no
doubt bitterly repented of—should involve the
detriment of others; for that M'Killop divined
the cause of Sir Roland's refusal he was thoroughly convinced. He replied, however—

"It is useless, Mr M'Killop; I cannot weigh
my birthright against your daughter's love; and
I have written to my uncle in such terms as to
make a reconciliation hopeless, even if I desired
it. No, that is out of the question; but I assure
you, from the bottom of my soul, that I consider
the sacrifice a very trifling one to make for Eila's
sake; and all I have got to do now, is to ask you
to sanction our marriage, regardless of Sir Roland
altogether."

"Not till you are reconciled—not till then, much as I like you, and because I like you much. What I can give is unreliable; it might go as it came—by a turn of the market; and then it would be on my conscience, God knows how heavily, that I had ruined you irretrievably. No, no; be reconciled first—first—and then——"

"I have told you already, Mr M'Killop, that it is impossible; Sir Roland's objections are insurmountable."

"Then, for the love of heaven, give up the engagement."

"Even that would not restore my birthright."

M'Killop covered his face with his hands, and remained thus, in profound thought, for some minutes; then rising, and, as if collecting all his fortitude to put the question, he said, in a steady voice—

"Be candid with me. Are you aware of the *precise* nature of Sir Roland's objection?"

"Yes, Mr M'Killop, I am."

"And it is?"

"It is too painful for me to mention; it would serve no purpose: his decision is unalterable."

"Bertrand, I have a *right* to know his reason; tell it to me frankly."

Bertrand hesitated for a moment, and then said, "Yes, Mr M'Killop, you *have* a right—I will give you his letter to read; here it is."

M'Killop took the letter, sat down, and read it through. The contents did not seem to surprise him; he made no exclamations; he read it through with quiet determination, and when he had finished, his voice and manner were calmer than they were when this interview began. Bertrand had not trusted himself to look at him, till he spoke.

"It was well I saw this—very well: do you believe the charge?"

This was a home-thrust for which Bertrand was not prepared; but, truthful to the core, he replied, "My uncle is so careful and accurate a man, that it did not occur to me to doubt it."

"And still you were willing to make such a connection?"

"I was—I am—as I have told you."

"You are not a worldly man, Bertrand; perhaps you may find your reward. This letter contains a truth, and yet not a truth. I was convicted, Bertrand, sentenced, and punished— all that is true; but I was an innocent man—I was no felon: do you believe me?"

" I—really—I——"

" No matter; it is as I say. I was made a
tool of by others in a design which, though legally
questionable, was, I believed, morally innocent.
Misfortune overtook me; appearances were against
me ; I was poor and friendless. I went to the
wall; those who might have saved me kept
silence and left me to my fate. The story is not
an uncommon one."

" But," exclaimed Bertrand, eagerly, " can this
not be righted now ? "

" Have patience. I underwent my term of
punishment, steadfastly adhering, through it all,
to a fixed resolution neither to despair nor to
succumb to the deteriorating influences of convict
life ; to do my duty to the utmost, and look forward to a reward, however distant. It came
sooner than I expected : my conduct was observed, and my partial release was obtained
earlier than usual. I procured a mercantile situation in the colony to which I had been banished,
and I prospered ; so that by the time my legal
term of punishment expired, I was on the high-
road to wealth. My subsequent conduct there
obliterated the marks of my antecedents. Many
others were similarly situated, and the considera-

tion of antecedents was not much in vogue. I
prospered and became rich; and then I carefully
considered whether or not I should take steps for
the vindication of my character at home. On
mature reflection I decided to let matters stand
as they were. I had good reason. I had changed
my name, you must know, before I began to be
known in the colony, and when my term of punishment had elapsed, and I had shifted to a distant part of another but adjacent colony, I changed
it again; and I hoped that when I returned
home a wealthy man, my identity with the poor
convict of forty years ago would never by any
chance be suspected, and that therefore it would
be unnecessary to rake up the old story and vin-
dicate myself. There would have been many
difficulties in doing so; and even if I had been
successful, many people would have remained
unconvinced, and the prison stigma would have
more or less remained with me. So I preferred
to start as an unknown man, having originally
sprung from the humblest origin, and having no
ties either of blood or of friendship to bind me
to the identity which I had lost. Only one man
in Scotland, to the best of my knowledge, was
aware of my secret. It had been necessary that

he should become aware of it professionally from some business connected with the transfer of property in the colony in which I had originally begun to prosper. He is no doubt the source of your uncle's information, although Sir Roland, from his intimacy with the colony, might possibly have become cognisant of my history independently. Still, as he alludes to an informant at home, this man is no doubt the man who, directly or indirectly, has supplied the information. On the whole, I am glad of this. It shows that my incognito has been otherwise preserved. That is my story—a sad one, is it not?"

"Deplorable," said Bertrand; "but you may right yourself yet."

"There is no necessity that I should do so, except for your sake, with your uncle; and that I hope I shall be able to do without any public scandal. I think you told me some time ago that Sir Roland was about to return home?"

"Yes, in a few weeks he will certainly leave the colony. His intention is to spend the spring at Pau."

"Very well, I will go there. I will wait for him there. When he arrives I will present myself to him and do my best to satisfy him. Probably I shall succeed; I think it probable that I shall induce him to withdraw his refusal; and as to what you have said to him in a moment of heat, why, he is a man of the world, and will not think the less of you in the long-run for a little spirit and impetuosity. Have you told Eila of his refusal?"

"Yes, I have."

"But not of its cause?"

"No, no; I would have done anything sooner."

"You are a gentleman, Bertrand: and what did she say? was she willing to take you penniless?"

"Oh, I am sure she was—of course she was; but she was agitated and overcome, and dwelt too much upon the sacrifice which she foolishly considered she would be entailing upon me, and in that way hung back a little, but it was only the result of the first shock of these deplorable news."

"Well, Bertrand, you have behaved perhaps recklessly, but, as a lover, nobly; and I would not have my girl not meet you half-way."

"She is an angel; and I have her love more fully far than I deserve."

" Very well ; and now, for the present, will
you agree to leave the case entirely in my
hands ? "

" Willingly."

" You may trust me to do my best."

" I am sure of it."

" But, in the mean time, we must not give his
Excellency a handle ; we must be all submis-
sion."

" Very well."

" And therefore there must be neither meeting
nor correspondence till I have seen him."

" O, that would be dreadful."

" It is necessary, however : if you put the
matter into my hands, I must manage it according to my own ideas."

And, after a long fight, Bertrand was fain to
consent to this. Under ordinary circumstances
he would have felt that the delay and his sub-
mission to his uncle were too heavy a price to
pay for Sir Roland's compliance ; but as it was
to clear Eila's birth from the stain of infamy, it
must, of course, be paid with fortitude.

" We shall go abroad for the spring months,"
continued M'Killop. " We may as well go
abroad at once and take up our abode at Pau.

When Sir Roland arrives, matters shall be righted at the earliest possible moment. And you must go back to your regiment and amuse yourself. The time will pass quickly enough."

" I may say 'good-bye' to Eila ? "

" No, no—better not; I'll explain it all to her,—that *I* am to reconcile Sir Roland, and that in the mean time we must be all fair and above-board in our obedience to his wishes. I'm sorry to part with you in this way, Bertrand; but keep up your heart. We shall all be happy together before long."

And so they parted; and Bertrand went homeward, sad, yet not despondent, and with a full belief that his intended father-in-law had all the heroic virtues of Jean Valjean, without any of that heroic criminal's shortcomings.

" I must be patient," he said; " I daresay the discipline is good for me; but oh! it will be very dreary without even a letter from her."

" That's a noble young fellow," muttered M'Killop to himself, when Bertrand had left him, "full of spirit and generosity; he shan't go to the wall: and if Sir Roland won't come to terms, the screw must be put on him—the screw—even if——"
The end of his sentence was not finished, however.

CHAPTER XXVIII.

When Bertrand reached his hotel, he found a letter, addressed to him in Eila's hand, lying on the hall-table. It had arrived only a few minutes before, the waiter said, so that she must have actually been writing it while he was with her father, unconscious of his presence in the hotel, and of the momentous interview going on below.

What luck it was, he thought, that she had written before an embargo was laid upon their correspondence! It was the last letter he could receive from her for a considerable time, and he must make the most of it; fortunately it seemed to be a long one. And so he betook himself to his room, to read it in the seclusion befitting so sacred an occupation. Eila was, as a rule, profuse in her epithets of endearment, and the commencement of her letters to Bertrand partook somewhat of an invocational character; but this letter was strangely barren of initial ornament, beginning simply " Dear Bertrand."

"A joke!" thought the reader, and went on.

" DEAR BERTRAND,—Though I suffer grievously both in body and in mind, I must nerve myself to write to you. I must collect all my strength and fortitude to do so—it is a task that will demand them all. Bertrand, I am going to do my *duty!* That word! how sad it is that it always sounds like a knell! I must do it, however, for your sake as for my own—my duty. Bertrand, all must now be over between us; what you told me to-day makes that inevitable. I must unsay any promise which I may weakly have allowed you to extract from me. I cannot consent to a clandestine marriage, or even to a secret correspondence—indeed I cannot. Duty to my father, openness, truth—these have always been my guiding principles. I cannot fall away from them—even for you. My father *positively refuses* his consent to our marriage without your uncle's sanction, and that can never be obtained now, as you have yourself said. Your own folly and rashness (it grieves me to use these reproachful expressions) have removed all such hopes.

But indeed my father says — and I quite feel
with him—that it would be beneath our dignity
to permit you to sue your uncle further. We
may not be aristocrats, but we have our proper
pride, and neither of us could consent to be placed
in such a humiliating position : therefore, Bertrand, you and I must do our best to forget the
past.   It has been very pleasant and bright, but,
alas ! all that is bright must fade.   Earthly happiness is fleeting and unstable, and this lesson we
must lay to heart, and try to profit by its salu-
tary pain.   Believe me, that if we face our trials
in a spirit of brave resignation, we shall find our
reward.   I have often had my misgivings during
our engagement—I will tell you so frankly now,
as it may be some consolation to you.   I have
often had my misgivings as to whether the mea-
sure of love which I could give you was an adequate return for the fervent affection which you
have professed.   I have had my doubts.   I have
often said to myself, ' Is this a summer-day love,
or will it stand, as well, the test of trouble, trial,
sorrow, and adversity ?   If it will not, it is not
the return which Bertrand's love merits.'

"I often tortured myself with these doubts.
To-day I have again closely examined my inmost

heart, and though there I find love for you, I cannot be at all sure that it is that kind of love which would be capable of consoling and supporting either you or myself in the circumstances under which marriage between us would now alone be possible. Therefore, perhaps, it is providential that that has happened which *has* happened; for if you had discovered, after marriage, that my love was not what it had seemed, you would have had bitterness in your heart against me all the days of your life. How could I have borne that?

"Very likely it is all for the best; I have at all events the satisfaction of feeling in my conscience that I am acting honestly and truthfully to you and to my father; and though I suffer keenly, I am supported by that feeling. Let us then forget the past. You will find many better and worthier of you than I am. Such disappointments wear off, they say, surprisingly soon, and very likely I shall hear of your marriage, and, I hope, happiness, before long. But you *must* make up matters with Sir Roland if possible. I must say your recklessness with regard to him has been *most* foolish; but when he knows that all is *quite* over between you and me, perhaps he will forgive and forget. I hope so. It will be unnecessary for you to see papa. A meeting would only be painful to you both. I have been with him ever since we parted, discussing this sad matter; and now I am writing this beside him, with his approval and sanction, and he shall read it before it is despatched. He thoroughly exonerates you, and desires me to express his good wishes. Now, farewell. Be happy, and forget, yours sincerely,   EILA M'KILLOP."

"Jupiter e cœlo perjuria ridet amantum." Very well for his Olympian majesty to laugh, who had the laugh usually on his own side, and very well for us who have outlived the "perjuria" in which, perhaps, some of us have had, let us hope passively, our share; but the sufferer who, in all his fresh youth and innocence, receives such a blow as this letter dealt to Bertrand Cameron, requires the strength of an Olympian to sustain the first effects of the shock. He received it in silence—not a word, not a cry escaped him. If you receive a musket - shot which wounds you not mortally, there is no end to your writhings, groans, and exclamations of pain; you tear up the grass, rend your garments, bite the stretcher, and execrate the surgeon; but the bullet which strikes the mortal blow lays you down calmly and quietly enough—a faint exclamation, a shiver, a gasp—and life is no longer there. The work has been done cleanly.

Thus when Bertrand received the letter from Sir Roland, his love was wounded deeply and painfully, and we all remember how vehement were his demonstrations; but now that he had read Eila's letter, he made no demonstrations, because his love was *dead*—pierced through and through, killed and slain on the spot—killed by a LIE. She might have loved him less than he had thought, she might have had less fortitude than he had believed, and still, albeit wounded, his love would have clung to her who dealt the wound, and still hoped for better times.

But a Lie! his love died before it, as by the stab of an assassin—died by murder,—

> " Murder most foul, as in the best it is,
> But this most foul, strange, and unnatural."

" A lie!" he muttered, as he crushed the letter in his grasp, and sat down silent, stern, motionless. His image of fine gold turned into most worthless clay, a world of bright hopes crumbled into dust and ashes, faith shattered, even dreamland dissolved, nothing left him but the reality of a cheated heart, no prospect between him and the horizon of his life, but a blank, empty wilderness, despoiled of every feature that yesterday had made it look so fair, even beneath the clouds; and all this transformation, all this ruin, wrought by the evil magic of a lie! How would he bear it? how could he bear it? He gave no outward indications. "While he was musing, the fire burned," no doubt, fiercely within him; but he sat perfectly silent and motionless, his gaze fixed on vacancy; sat on, hour after hour, till darkness deepened into night, and his room was only lighted by the gleam of a street-lamp flaring drearily through the window. At last he became gradually conscious of a continued knocking at the door, and roused himself, looked about confusedly as if he had been asleep and dreaming, then rose and opened the door. A waiter — somewhat ill-pleased at having been kept so long waiting, and perhaps disappointed to find that the sensation of discovering Bertrand hanging to his bed-post was denied him—proved to be the knocker.

"Gentleman down-stairs for you, sir; particularly anxious to see you, sir. Thought you was asleep, sir; thought you was—didn't know *what* to think, sir."

"Never mind, I'll follow you; go on."

"This way, sir; coffee-room, sir," and Bertrand walked mechanically into it.

CHAPTER XXIX.

THE room was occupied by two gentlemen, one unknown to Bertrand, but the other was Mr Coppinger of the —th.

"Good morning," said that gentleman, affably. "I've ki-called to make it all square with you."

"Oh," said Bertrand, still in a dream. "Oh, indeed? but I don't quite understand."

"You're not s-savage, are you?"

"Not at all; why should I be?"

"Well, you know, I was a little fi-flustered last night, and je-jealous, and savage, I suppose, and wanted to call you out; only you wouldn't wait for L-arkins. Don't you remember? Ah! perhaps you were too ski-crewed?"

"No; I remember something about it now."

"I've referred it to Larkins (let me introduce my friend L-arkins of the —th), and he's certain I was in the wrong. Very likely I was.

I s-s-sometimes am; but, when I am, I ap-pop-pologise. I 'pologise now. Accept my a-pop-pop—— ?"

"Certainly," said Bertrand. "I bear no malice."

"That's right; here's my hand." And they shook hands over it.

"D-doing anything to-night?" continued the Kicker.

Doing anything to-night! Bertrand's every motive of action was so entirely paralysed that the idea of spontaneous action, of his having any will on any subject, or any existence apart from passive suffering, sounded strange to him; but he answered that he didn't think he had anything to do that evening.

"Dine with me then at the —— ki-Club. Some of the regiment who have relieved us are ki-coming. They ain't like us, you know, but I daresay they won't pick your pock-ockets. Is it a fi-fixture?"

Bertrand reflected for a moment. After all, why should he stay moping by himself? He should go mad if he did; not that that signified, of course—nothing signified now; but he might as well dine with this fellow: it would help to keep thought away, at all events, for an hour or two; and so he agreed.

"Eight sharp," said the Kicker; and then, stepping back from the door, remarked,—"I say, how you took me in! I thought it was a ki-case between you and Miss MacCollop; it l-looked dey-evilish like it; but I expect I was rather t-ight; and she says it's all humbug, and that you're only ki-common friends."

"There is nothing between us, you may depend upon that," said Bertrand.

"I know that now, and at first I thought there ki-couldn't be; she laughs so fi-furiously at in-fantry—no of-fence to you, old fellow; it's a way gi-girls have; can't help it, I expect. I've been having tea there just now; it was awfully jolly; she's as sp-spooney as an owl on me. Rum old thing the mother! Angling, L-arkins says; but trust ki-Coppinger to dodge the h-ook. Bye, bye; eight sharp."

A bitter smile crossed Bertrand's face as the hussar left the room. "It would be a just retribution," he said to himself, "if she only had a heart, that it should be trampled under foot by a travesty of a man like this fellow. Pshaw! I'll think no more of her, or any woman. Pigott's right after all. I'll stick to his maxim for the future. Broken hearts are all very well for the stage. Hearts don't break in real life. Mine shan't" (with a sort of hysterical gasp), "and I don't feel a bit down on my luck now. In a week I shall be perfectly jolly, and go back to the good old soldiering life, and to men and friends—men who are always true. How my head aches! Champagne will cure that, though! and my imbecile host is good so far, at all events." With which complimentary reflection on the genial Kicker, he went to dress, feeling a strange, tight pain across the forehead, but a' rising exhilaration of spirits. "What an extraordinary-looking fellow I am!" he cried, as he looked in the glass; "my eyes look twice their usual size, and ten times as bright as usual. Ha! ha! ha! it's really most absurd! What spirits I'm in! No one would think that——Oh, hang all women!

> ' Merrily, merrily march away,
>   Soldier's glory lives in story;
>   His laurels are green when his locks are grey.
>   Hurrah for the life of a soldier!'"

and he kept singing the refrain of the devil-may-care old marching-song till he was dressed, trolling it lustily as he drove along to the Club, and only suppressing it with an effort, in compliment to that institution, when he entered its walls. It was quite astonishing, he kept remarking to himself, what spirits he was in.

The party consisted of some half-a-dozen gentlemen—Coppinger, Larkins, and the promised contingent from the new regiment—rather stolid-looking young men, on the whole, with a sealed-pattern look about the face, collars, and other features, suggesting the idea that they had been run up on contract by the same firm, and not promising great things in the way of an intellectual evening. It is wonderful, however, what miracles champagne will effect on such occasions; it not only loosens tongues, but induces a bland feeling of toleration for whatever platitudes they may utter. And so, after two or three rounds of the magical fluid, the party was as noisy and convivial as need be. The *quantity* of talk was at all events undeniable, and the laughter boisterous—evidently kindling the wrath of several greybeards dotted about the dining-room, and who were topping up their frugal repasts with jorums of whisky-punch, through the fumes of which many a jaundiced glance was cast upon the proceedings of the banqueters.

Coppinger naturally became at once the butt of the party, and the smallest jackdaw had a peck at that bird of gorgeous plumage. He bragged about himself, his regiment, his horses, his clothes, cigars, and conquests. He was trotted out on all these subjects, and stepped out bravely, inspiring the mildest tyro in the art of chaff, supplied by the new regiment, with a notion that he (the tyro) was "going it," and no mistake, and that his brother officers, in mess assembled, must be shown, at the earliest possible opportunity, what an unsuspected magazine of wit and banter they possessed in him. But Bertrand was the life of the party; he never flagged; his spirits rose to the wildest exuberance. Story after story, sally after sally, flowed from him in a sparkling stream; and when, dinner being over, and the greybeards gone, he proposed the Kicker's health, it was in a serio-comic speech of such grotesque fun, that the house fairly " came down"—in more senses than one, indeed, for angry seniors descended from the reading-room to remonstrate. The Kicker himself was loudest in his plaudits, confiding to a neighbour in a hiccupy whisper, " This ki-codger is a deal too good for the Fi-feet, you know ; *we* must have him. I've got my eye on him, mark you ; and, ki-cost what it may, he comes to us. Lord bless you ! he could give most of us a stone in the way of chaff. Talk of bi-Belcher of the Blues ! bi-Belcher's a baby to ki-Cameron."

The party did not conclude their festivities in the dining-room ; eventually an adjournment to the smoking-room took place, where their loud merriment soon left them a clear field ; and there they " made a night of it." Scarcely a Club rule escaped infraction. Supper was ordered up and procured by menaces ; bones, and more bones, and yet again bones. Songs, choruses, and view-holloas echoed through the outraged halls ; and in the lulls between the grander salvoes, the popping of champagne and soda-water corks indicated the process of priming and loading for new efforts. Bertrand still led the orgies ; it was under his direction that the fun grew faster and more furious. By degrees a certain enfeeblement crept over some of the revellers ; certain legs began to decline the per-pendicular ; certain voices began to stray hope-

lessly up and down the gamut in search of a
practicable key-note. Men might be seen dropping their tumblers on the floor, and making
elaborate apologies to the fragments ; and a
proposal on the part of the Kicker to· " draw"
the sleeping members of the Club, only escaped
execution from the difficulties of "getting up
the hill" (the brandy-and-soda equivalent for
the staircase).

But there was no enfeeblement about Bertrand ; his spirits never flagged. The wine,
which he drank in bumpers, never sent him
beyond the level he had been on all the evening.
Again and again he rallied the drooping forces ;
again and again repelled the remonstrances of
the Club-master ; again and again scouted the
idea of turning out. Coppinger—who looked at
all times the very incarnation of strong waters—
beyond several attempts to press a shilling into
Bertrand's hand, with a view, it was surmised,
to securing him for the mounted branch of the
service, did not betray that he was seriously in-
convenienced by his liberal potations, and man-
fully seconded Bertrand's efforts to keep the ball
rolling. But at last a time came when the
ball would roll no farther. The bravest sub of

horse or foot is but mortal, and, like other
mortals, has his gauge. A pretty general collapse took place, and Bertrand and Coppinger
retired together from the stricken field, carrying
off their slain in the shape of Larkins—not without difficulty, that gentleman's "ma-chinery," as
Coppinger characterised his legs, being "all
nohow." As for the others, two at least were
left to be swept up by the servants in the morning—the Kicker contemptuously remarking, with
a jerk of his thumb in the direction of their prostrate forms, — "Never saw such form for ki-
cavalry. Hang me if they're even fit for the
Engineers! ki-carry nothing — the di-duffers!"
He apologised for Larkins's state of dilapidation
by explaining that his "stomjack" was out of
order—the result of an unusually protracted
trial, incident to a change of quarters, which up
to this moment it had undergone most creditably
—adding, however, that he would have left him
there without compunction, if it wasn't that they
were both due in York on the following forenoon, and it would be slow work travelling without him. They reached the hotel as the bleak
winter morning was beginning to dawn. Coppinger asked Bertrand as to his plans. Bertrand

hadn't thought of them ; but he was ready for anything.

"Come with us to York? I'll put you up, and sh-ow you what a regiment *can* be made."

"All right," said Bertrand ; "when does the train start?"

"Ten o'clock ; we'll put in an hour or two of sleep, then a de-evilled kidney, a brandy-and-soda, and off you go."

"I'll be ready ; but I don't feel sleepy. I'll take a walk and see the beauties of the place, ha! ha! Please tell the people to have my things put up." And Bertrand strode away down the street. The Kicker gazed after him in hazy admiration.

"Fi-form, by Jove! Pace and form! L-ost on in-fantry! quite lost ; but I've got my eye on him, so just you wait a bit." With which consolatory reflection, addressed to an adjacent lamp-post, the Kicker nodded his head sapiently, and turned into the hotel.

Bertrand was not sleepy ; he felt as if nothing could ever make him sleepy again. A wild exhilaration still possessed him—a desire for rapid motion, bustle, and noise. At the moment he would have been the very man for a forlorn-hope or a reckless charge. Everything was a glorious whirl in his brain. No dull thoughts of grief were there. Wild incongruous absurdities presented themselves to his mind, and made him laugh aloud ; fragments of last night's songs rose to his lips, and he shouted them in the empty streets.

Pursuing his random walk, he chanced to pass the M'Killops' hotel. At sight of it, he seemed to be touched by some exquisitely humorous thought, and his laughter rang loud and high under their windows — no bitter, self-mocking laughter, but blithe and hearty peals of merriment ; and so he passed on and on ; and the sun rose, and the town became broad awake, and the streets filled, and the strange glances of the passers-by delighted him as something irresistibly comic and absurd ; and so, in the highest glee, he arrived at the hotel, just in time to dress, and start with his two companions, both showing considerable symptoms of wear and tear, for the train.

"I'll tell you what it is, Kicker," cried Bertrand, "it's a deal too slow going to York ; I can't do it, old fellow. I don't think I could stand the smell of the stables just now. I'll go on to town, and perhaps run over to Paris to-morrow ; will you come ?"

The Kicker could not, but he honoured the sudden change of plans and the wholly insufficient reasons given for it, as a new indication of " form," and so let Bertrand off his engagement easily.

During the journey Bertrand sang and rattled on like a maniac ; and nothing but his appreciation of the " form " thereby indicated would have prevented the Kicker from feeling a good deal bored by his new friend, being, to use his own expression, not a little " jumpy " this morning. As for Larkins, he and his " stomjack " had made no very perceptible rally, and were travelling as, more or less, the luggage and personal effects of Lieutenant Coppinger.

At York, the latter gentleman, after carefully collecting Larkins, left the train, bidding Bertrand adieu with affectionate *empressement*, and an assurance that his eye was, and would continue to be, on him ; and so we shall leave Bertrand for a little while he pursues his journey.

CHAPTER XXX.

WE know a good deal about Eila now, and not
much to her advantage ; but we shall not
moralise over her, or set ourselves to trace by
what process of thought she had decided to write
that letter to Bertrand which had produced such
exhilarating effects upon him : whether she had
once loved him, and, having loved, had tired of
him ; whether she had never loved him at all,
but only his future prospects, and so thrown him
over when they seemed lost ; or whether some
new and violent attraction (scarcely the Kicker,
surely !) had suddenly possessed her. Into such
speculations we shall not enter ; suffice it that
she had written what she had written, and com-
mitted herself by the clumsy and unladylike
expedient of a falsehood. That Nemesis over-
takes all crime in some shape or other is the
orthodox belief—and in this instance the ortho-

dox belief was justified. Her letter had barely reached its destination, when Nemesis was down upon her, "wanting" her for the little fiction which it contained. A message came from her father that he wished particularly to see her at once, and she went down to him. His manner was grave, but neither gloomy nor depressed.

"I have seen Bertrand," he said. This was startling to begin with, and rather threw her off her balance.

"When?" she asked faintly, wondering if he could possibly have received her letter and communicated its contents to her father already.

"He only left me a quarter of an hour ago." Eila breathed again. "He has told you of his uncle's refusal?" continued her father.

"Oh yes."

"And of what he has done?"

"Yes, indeed; he has been most foolish."

"Still I should scarcely have expected you to make the admission."

"Indeed, papa, I am more sensible than you imagine."

"Humph! but you were willing to marry him?"

"Never without your permission, dear papa."

“ And that you shall have, my child, I trust.”

“ What ! ” cried Eila, in an agitation which her father mistook for joy.

“ You must not be too sanguine, my dear, but I hope to be in a position to sanction it before long.”

“ Oh ! but——but——”

“ But what, Eila ? ” said her father, looking at her in surprise.

“ Sir Roland will *never* give his consent, papa.”

“ What does that matter, if you only wait for mine ? ”

“ True,” said Eila, with despair in her heart and the ghost of a smile on her face, which had become very pale—“ true.”

“ However,” M‘Killop continued, “ mine is still dependent upon his.”

“ Yes, papa,” murmured Eila.

“ In the mean time you must promise me not to have any sort of communication with Bertrand.”

The promise was given with most filial alacrity.

“ I think—mind I only say, I think—I shall be able to get over Sir Roland’s objections.”

"Oh, papa!" gasped Eila; "how can you?"

"Never mind how; I think I can; but don't be too sanguine."

"I won't! I won't!"

"There is a reasonable prospect of success, and no call to despair—that's all."

"Thank you, papa."

"A month or two will settle it all; meantime you must try to be as happy as you can. It is all to be worked out by me, without any communication with Bertrand — that's part of the conspiracy, ha! ha!—and you may rely upon my using every effort, and making any sacrifice for you both. Bertrand is a noble fellow; you will be lucky if you become his wife. Now run away, my dear; I must be busy."

And Eila went back to her room, feeling rather like a person who has inadvertently punched an unstopable hole in the bottom of his boat far out at sea. "How could I be so mad as to write that letter?" so ran her reflections. "I might have waited twenty-four hours, at all events. Now, if Sir Roland gives his consent, what is to happen? Good heavens! what *will* happen? Bertrand *must* know that I have told him a fib about papa. What will he think

of me ?" and at the reflection her face tingled
with shame. "I wish I had kept a copy of it;
I'm pretty sure, though, that it could not be
explained away. It was too broad. Why *did*
I make it so broad? Goose! Oh, dear! oh,
dear! how he will despise me! What *shall* I
do?" and she wrung her hands in sheer despair.
Nemesis had it all her own way for a little.
"And if," Eila went on thinking,—"if the consent *did* come! fancy losing him—such a match!
all for this foolish, abominable, stupid, useless,
little fib! Oh, dear! oh, dear! I deserve to be
poisoned for my clumsiness." After a little,
though, and all of a sudden, a brighter view
dawned on Eila, and she started up and clapped
her hands with delight. "I have it!" she cried;
"I have it! I'll tell Bertrand that I told the
fib all for his sake—merely to prevent him from
ruining himself by marrying me; that I did my
best to alienate and disgust him with me, for his
own sake, out of my generosity and love for him.
Bertrand *is* such a goose, I don't think he can
possibly refuse to take it all in. No fear; I'll
whistle him back, and he'll come, with thanks
and apologies." And she laughed gleefully at
the prospect. "What a piece of good fortune

that correspondence is forbidden ! was ever anything so lucky? I can never be sufficiently
thankful for that. But what papa's chances are,
I don't understand ; still he never speaks with
such confidence, unless he is pretty certain.
Meantime, Eila, my dear, keep your spirits up ;
it will all come right somehow ; and if any good
chance offers in the mean time, why, Master
Bertrand, you mayn't get me yet." And the
airy unsophisticated young creature went lilting
gaily down to the drawing-room ; and Nemesis
went home again—for a space.

CHAPTER XXXI.

Two nights after we left Bertrand *en route* for London, Pigott was sitting in his barrack-room, deep in the recesses of the cosiest of chairs, before the brightest of fires, smoking the most fragrant of cabanas.

It was all but his usual hour for going to bed, and he was grappling with the problem whether it would bore him most to rise and let his dog in at once, or to endure his scratchings and whinings at the door, till he got up, at any rate, to go to bed. Having apparently " concluded" to let the dog scratch, and having decided that the boredom of a dog generally isn't compensated for by any pleasure he affords, his thoughts branched gradually from the canine, to the human, bore, and to the reflection how Bertrand Cameron had bored him lately, and what a relief it was that he was away—for a bit.

" I don't know, after all," he amended, on

continued reflection, " that it *is* any comfort.
One misses the beggar, somehow. I suppose
that incessant irritation has some sort of a—
what d'ye call it ?—stimulating effect. I daresay I should be glad enough if Bertrand was
sitting there at this moment. It's habit, I suppose. Besides, I should like to know how this
business of his is getting on. Hang it! there's
the lamp going out next! I won't get up,
though. *Let* it go out; there's lots of fire. *I*
don't care." He spoke bitterly, as if the lamp
was going out from personal *animus* against him,
and as if his resignation would mortify it. " But
a saint couldn't stand *this* now !" he cried, starting up a little later. His dog was barking furiously outside the door, and some one was apparently baiting him—some one who danced about,
with whooping, and shouting, and laughter.
Pigott strode rapidly to the door, and threw it
open with a bang. His dog rushed in past him,
cowed and trembling, and a tall figure, stepping
out of the darkness, shouted with grotesque
gesticulations—

> " ' Mastiff, greyhound, mongrel grim,
> Hound or spaniel, brach or lym,
> Or bobtailed tyke, or trundle-tail,
> Tom will make them weep and wail!'

Yes, that he will.   Hand him over, in the King's name!   Your dog, your dog; my kingdom for your dog!"

"What in the devil's name is all this?" cried Pigott.   "Bertrand Cameron! by all that's sinful!   Why — what!   Good heavens, man! are you drunk?"

"Drunken with youth, but not a drop of wine!" and Bertrand stalked into the room, revealing to his astonished friend a face pale as marble, from which his great dark eyes seemed to stand out as if bursting with the lurid fire that shone through them.   His dress was all in disorder, and his whole aspect ghastly and appalling.

"Good heavens, Bertrand!" cried Pigott, starting back, "what has happened to you?"

"Of all men else I have avoided thee," was the reply, still in the stage-struck manner; "yet why not thou as well's another?   Caitiff, I thirst!   Bring me a goblet of nectar, dashed with the waters of Pharpar, Abana, and the Oxus!"

"Wait a minute," said Pigott, leaving the room, "and you shall have it.   The Oxus, did you say?"

"Strong of the Oxus."

"All right."   And he was off, and ten minutes

after, poor Bertrand was lying on his back in bed, held down by four of the strongest men in the regiment.

"Brain-fever," said the doctor to Pigott, as he left the room. "These fellows mustn't take their eyes off him for a minute. See that they're properly relieved; and call me if there's anything special wanted. He's as strong as an elephant, and he and the fever will have a jolly good round. Five to two on Cameron, though. Goodnight."

Poor Bertrand! The hardest might feel some pity for him now, as he lay there, wrecked and shattered, all his sufferings personified by the weird magic of delirium, and hovering about him —a sleepless army of visionary foes. It was a cruel deed that had brought him to this, slaying his love, eclipsing his faith, mocking a heart infinitely true and trusting, and robbing it of these "first joys that come not back again." Exalted loyalty and stainless truth were the very essence of his character; and his love, like Sir Galahad's strength, was as the love of ten, "because his heart was pure." It was a cruel apocalypse for such a nature, when his ideal appeared with "a lie in her right hand." It

was a cruel death for such a love to die—
poisoned by the impurity of that to which it
clung. As for her who had done the deed, perhaps Pigott might almost be forgiven the ener-
getic anathema which he awarded to her, as he
sat watching by her victim's side, surely divining
the story of his plight. It was brief, incisive,
and to the point, as his utterances were wont
to be.

The doctor's prediction proved true; the
struggle between Bertrand's splendid vigour of
frame and the fever was long and fierce. Day
after day passed, and still the battle raged, with
now and then an armistice of lethargy, but never
one gleam of coherent consciousness.

Day after day, the dark eyes—seeming to grow
ever darker and larger—stared with a hunted
look of anxiety and dread, or blazed with the
fire of frenzy. Day and night the parched lips
moved unceasingly, moaning piteous remonstrances, or shouting fierce defiance—chanting some
scrap of a tuneless song, muttering some fragment of a prayer, or whispering a haunting name
or number, in weariful iterations; day and night
doomed to utter every waif and stray from the
chaos of the mind, to repeat every echo from the

hurly-burly of the brain. Day after day passed, and still the fever held its ground, and poor Bertrand lay, as lost to life and use as Merlin in the hollow oak, imprisoned by his false enchantress, with the spell of "woven paces and of waving arms." Through all this weary ordeal Pigott's devotion never flagged ; allowing himself a very minimum of rest and change, he was by his friend's side at all times when not absolutely required for regimental duty. Watching and supervising, a very terror to *laissez-aller* hospital orderlies and sluggish "fatigue-men," the sybarite forgot his roses, the typical "selfish beggar" of the regiment forgot himself. Ungrudging and ungrumbling, he went about his labour of love in the same quiet practical way in which he was wont to cherish himself; and he did more than he would have done for himself, for he restricted and denied himself in everything that might have hindered his efficiency as a nurse. The secret, perhaps, was, that what are called "unexpansive natures" gain in concentration what they lose in expansiveness. They are less ornamental ; they do not fill the eye and challenge public admiration ; they are not for ever posturing in benign attitudes ; but for steadfast thoroughness, when once their feelings have made way through the unpromising crust, commend us to them rather than the others—the " sympathetic natures." The spaniel is all things delightfully to all men, and true to none; but the churl of a bull-dog—there is nothing to beat his loyalty to his single friend. No outsider shall share his manger, though there is room in it for ten; but he would die for his friend if occasion was, and he only knew how. To his brother officers, not given to ethical speculation, Pigott was a wonder.

"Given up his whist, you know," cried one. "And his billiards," cried another. " And his rackets," "And his hunting," "And his champagne," "And sleeps in his clothes," all in an ascending scale of astonishment. " And yet how he grumbled about Bertrand's boring him with his love-affair!" " Said he must exchange to get away from it." " Awfully queer fellow, Pigott." "Selfish beast, though, all the same; positively refused to take my duty on Saturday, to let me go out hunting!—pretended he couldn't leave Bertrand!" " Rubbish!" " Selfish to the backbone." One or two voices, indeed, would be raised against the theory of Pigott's selfishness, but the general sentiment favoured it. And yet probably there were not many in that self-abnegating circle of young men who would have done what Pigott was doing for his friend. There is nothing so selfish as your society of "awfully good fellows," who are for ever exclaiming against the selfishness of their neighbours; and nowhere are there more real Levites, than where every one is, *ex officio*, as it were, an honorary good Samaritan.

At last the crisis of the fever came—the grand final struggle between the antagonists. It came; it was intense and protracted, and it seemed doubtful if Bertrand could come out of it alive; or, if alive, with his reason unimpaired. But it passed, and the patient fell into a long and gentle sleep—the signal and the assurance of his victory. It was a moment of sincere happiness for Pigott when at last he heard his name uttered, in a scarcely audible voice, from the bed, and, drawing aside the curtain, found that his friend was awake and conscious.

"Where am I, Pigott?"

"At home, in your own barrack-room, old fellow."

"Oh, yes, I see;" but his eyes wandered

about in a questioning way; the world of reality seemed dim and strange to him after the vivid phantasmagoria of his long delirium.

"Is there no parade to-day? I feel as if I had been asleep for an age."

"You've been very ill, but you're all right now, Bertrand; only you must be very quiet. Don't speak, but try to sleep."

"Very ill! yes, yes—why, I can't even lift my hand! I declare I can't move! How odd it is! Turn me away from the light, please; I'll go to sleep again, if you're quite certain there's no parade."

"Not an atom of a parade."

And Pigott turned him, and he slept long and deep, and woke the next time stronger, and quite comprehending that he had been dangerously ill, though he said nothing, as yet, of the cause. And so he passed through the first stages of his recovery, sleeping much, and lying silent when awake—scarcely speaking, indeed, except to express a want—querulously enough, as the wont of convalescents is. And Pigott still stuck to his post, and nursed him zealously through this most trying period to nurses, displaying a gentleness and consideration truly wonderful, but which would have been still more astonishing in a professed philanthropist, perhaps.

And so the weeks rolled on, and Bertrand still continued silent on the subject of his love-catastrophe, which to his friend appeared a satisfactory symptom. "It shows, at any rate, that the thing's at an end," he would say to himself; "if it hadn't been, he would never have kept off the subject so long. It's a great comfort—it was a horrid bad business. The girl is as hollow as a drum, and her governor a snob compared with our big-drummer. It's a blessing it's at an end; but I wish I saw the old boy a little cheerier. That will come in time, though. He must have change of air and scene, and all that sort of thing, as soon as he can be moved." The doctor quite fell in with this latter view, and by-and-by Bertrand got a couple of months' sick-leave, and went down to Bournemouth accompanied by his faithful friend.

"It is my own case, you see," Pigott explained, as if apologising for his devotion; "and I'm not going to let him out of my hands till he'll do me credit."

CHAPTER XXXII.

THE spring was well advanced, the season was
an early one, and the weather was glorious as
summer; and in such circumstances, Bournemouth is a charming place to those who come, as
Bertrand did, to drink in health and vigour from
its pure but genial air. The woods, where,
among the much-prevailing pines, their monot-
ony was relieved by less sombre trees, were beginning to wrap themselves in that wonderful
soft green mist—if one may so express it—when
the foliage is just being wooed from the bud by
spring's caresses; and everywhere the primrose
ran riot, and, mingling with early wild-flowers of
other hues, lettered spring's advent gloriously in
grove and lane, on slope and meadow; and the
sun shone constantly, and the sky was clear and
blue, and the sea, reflecting all, lay sleeping
underneath the sunny cliffs, peaceful and motion-

less for days. It was a delicious time for all men, but for an invalid the days came "with healing on their wings," and Bertrand regained his strength rapidly. He and Pigott were established in quarters on the eastern cliff; and they could not have been better placed, for the aspect was southern, and the sea lay at their feet. On one hand they looked upon the Isle of Wight, with its constant strange transformations of light and shade wrought by the sea-mists and the sun; and on the other to the graceful outlines of the Dorsetshire coast, sweeping round to form the western enclosure of the bay. But it was to the sea Bertrand constantly looked; the contemplation of its vastness and calm soothed his lacerated spirit, and, gazing at the far-away sea-horizon, he drank in unconsciously that indefinable sense of promise and hope which it always suggests. It was very good for him to be there; the companionship of the sea was very good for him. Pigott was indeed a little disappointed to find that his abstraction did not abate very much, and that his efforts to divert his mind to what was going on about him, or to amuse him with everyday subjects, continued to be but very partially successful; yet the return of health

and strength, the pure air, and " the lessons of
the sea," were surely, if slowly, doing their work.
Never, indeed, might the elastic joyousness of
youth before its first check return to him—never
again the same simplicity of faith—never again
those early dreams of the heart that make a
fairy-land of life. But all these things go necessarily in the tear and wear of the world; it is
only a matter of time—simply a question between a sudden lopping off and a gradual process
of grinding away with a file. The end of our
·hird decade sees the last of them, one way or
other. And as for the permanent effects of love-
disappointments beyond this limit, does any one
now believe in them ? Does any one believe that
any nature not afflicted with some grave moral
or intellectual flaw, will have its capacity for
work, usefulness, sympathy, and even enjoyment,
paralysed for ever by any such agency ?

Not very long ago it would have been held a
kind of blasphemy against " the higher sensibilities " to hold such language. A few generations
back it was quite a venial offence to be useless,
worthless, or at least disagreeable, for the remain-
der of your days, if you had only been disappointed in love : it was expected of you, indeed,

by the romantic. But from that affectation, at least, let us be thankful that our age is free, and that the disappointed lover is no longer under any sort of necessity either to become a respectable cynic, the pest and scourge of his associates, or to go drunk to destruction at a hand-gallop, *viâ* the dirty sloughs of the vulgarest Bohemianism.

We give the hapless lover our sympathy, and a reasonable time to "wax well of his deep hurt;" but we know perfectly well that a time arrives when the reality of his suffering comes to an end, and when any farther demonstration thereof becomes fictitious and dramatic. For his own, and Pigott's sake, may this time soon come to Bertrand, and we should be disappointed in him, if we found him wearing the willow thereafter.

Time passed on; the two months' leave drew towards a close; Bertrand's health was almost quite restored, and he was on the fair way to be very soon fit to return to his old duties and pursuits: but never, all this time, had he spoken to his friend of Eila, or his recent engagement, or the catastrophe which had terminated it. Pigott was not only very inquisitive about it (although

this he would have scorned to admit), but he had
formed an idea—to which the wish, perhaps, was
father—that Bertrand's health and spirits would
both be materially benefited by an unbosoming of
himself; and so he now never lost an opportunity
of giving him "a lead over" when any event or
turn of the conversation suggested an opening.
It was in vain, however, that Pigott skirmished
or "showed the way;" Bertrand was evidently
not going to be manœuvred into a confidence,
and he still refrained from volunteering one.
There is not a great deal to be done at Bournemouth.   Fine air, sunshine, blue skies, the beautiful sea, the bursting foliage, the glories of the
spring—these are all very well for a dreamer or
an invalid ; they were all very well for Bertrand
as yet, and he was contented with sitting in the
open air, strolling along the cliffs and among the
pine-woods, or now and then undergoing an hour
or so of modified dislocation on a hired "animal."
But for Pigott, who was a man of action, and in
his normal state went in for everything, his friend
began to feel that Bournemouth must be very
slow indeed ; and at last he begged him not to
sacrifice any more of his leave to him.   He was
all right now, he said, and would get on famously

by himself, and probably rejoin the regiment in a
fortnight. But Pigott refused to desert his friend.
" No, no," he said; " I'll stick to you till I land
you on the duty-rolster again. I take a pride in
my case, you see. If I went away you would be
hipped and moped, and ten to one you would
have a relapse, and I might have all this business
over again. We're doing very well; we'll take
some more camel exercise to-morrow; and, by
the by, I was forgetting—I've found a friend—a
lady friend, here. I met her this morning when
I was struggling with that thief of a butcher in
his shop—romantic spot for a meeting !—I went
to point out to him that, though ignorant of an-
atomy generally, I was aware that sweetbreads
and liver are not identical—not even in value—
which he seemed to fancy. She, it appeared,
had come to annihilate him with some similar
sarcasm; but we met, and our wrath vanished.
The butcher still survives."

" Who is your friend ? "

" A very jolly sort of woman; I knew her in
India. She is the wife, or the widow, of one
Curtis, who commanded a native infantry regi-
ment at Benares when we were there, years ago.
I wonder whether she *is* wife or widow now; no

interested motives—she's fifty if she's a day, and could no more get into your chair than the hippopotamus;—but it's awkward not knowing. Curtis's habits were certainly not calculated to lengthen life, still I think he must be alive."

"Well, what about the lady?"

"Oh, only that I met her, and we were very glad to see each other; and I was refreshed by hearing the old Hindoo jargon again—the *lingua Franca* which native infantry used to talk, you know; and she wanted me to go to 'tiffin,' and I told her I had to go back to you; and she asked about you, and your illness, and your name; and when I mentioned the musical word 'Cameron,' she snuffed the heather, and asked if you were from Scotland; and when I said I feared you were, she sprang upon me—morally, that is—and said that she too hailed from that fortunate country—information which her application of the term 'imparrtinent' to me, rendered superfluous; but when she found that you really were a true-born Celt, she was much interested, and said, 'Bring him to dinner, to-night:' and now, will you come?"

"My dear fellow, it is impossible—quite impossible."

"Why?"

"Because it is. I'm not up to it. You must go by yourself."

"You don't know what you're missing, Bertrand. Her maiden name, she tells me, was 'M'Kascal.' Can you resist *that?*"

"I must indeed. Did you promise for me?"

"I said I would try to bring you."

"Well, you must go yourself, and make my apologies. It will be a change for you, after moping with a sick man for weeks;" and Pigott finally agreed to go, and went.

The evening might have passed rather heavily for Bertrand, thus left to himself, but when the post came in, it brought him something which effectually rescued him from *ennui,* at all events —a letter addressed in a handwriting well known, and once inexpressibly dear to him. At sight of it, his heart beat so violently that he gasped for breath; and his hand so shook that he was unable to tear open the envelope. He was still, we must remember, but a convalescent. "What a fool I am!" he muttered to himself, at last. "As if anything could alter the past! Nothing short of a revelation from heaven could make me believe in truth from that hand again! So, what does it matter to me what the contents of the letter are?" He then opened, and read as follows:—

"Pau, *May* 186—.

"MY OWN DEAREST BERTRAND,—Man proposes, but God disposes. When I wrote my last sad letter to you, in which I seemed to sign away my very life, I was proposing to secure your ultimate happiness—your prosperity, at all events. In doing so I was prepared to sacrifice myself in every way, and this I did. I do not boast of it. I would do it again for your dear sake. I even deceived you a little for your own good. I even sacrificed what was dearer to me than life—the truth. Ah, Bertrand! I fear I am sadly wicked. I fear you are dearer to me than the truth. I sacrificed it for you, and I belied my own love that you might rather even think me unworthy than that *I* should be the destroyer of your fortunes. I wrote that letter with my heart's blood, and I have never smiled since—never, at least, till yesterday. But a merciful Providence has seen fit to remove the burden from me which was heavier than I could bear. I send you news —joyful news—glorious news. It has pleased

Providence so to dispose the heart of that dear, excellent man, your uncle, that he no longer objects to our *union*. Everything else seems to go from me as I write these words, and I can only see my beloved Bertrand standing before me, claiming me as his *bride!* and he shall not claim in vain. Come to me, my own—come quickly; every moment without you is an agony. Yes, Bertrand, papa had a *long, delightful* interview with Sir Roland yesterday; and he has agreed to *everything*. We are to have *enough* in the mean time; and he says he has no intention of marrying, and that *we are to be his heirs!* Is it not too much happiness? I said to you in jest once that if he only saw *me*, all his objections would fade away! A conceited speech, was it not? But, dearest, I do really flatter myself that I have had *something* to do with this blessed turn of affairs; and it is my pride and joy that I have been able to serve my beloved Bertrand's interests. His Excellency was *immensely* taken with me. (Don't be jealous.) I could see *that* at once; and, under Providence, I believe I have been the instrument of softening his heart.

"But I will not talk of that now. We shall laugh over all our troubles and adventures soon —shall we not?

"And now, dearest, come, come, come! Papa says 'Come;' Sir Roland says 'Come;' and *I* say 'COME!' in the largest capitals. If you can get leave, we might be married here, and then have a ramble in the Pyrenees. What a heavenly programme! In that case I would get my *trousseau* in Paris. Might we not meet there, and then come back to this place, which, *from yesterday*, will always be dear to me? His Excellency, who is *far from strong*, I grieve to say, cannot venture on England till the summer is well advanced; and as he *must* be at the wedding, this place would suit all parties best. Write—telegraph—let me hear from you *on the instant*—best of all, telegraph to say, 'I am starting,' and then start at once. And now a short farewell, my beloved Bertrand.—Your own fond, hoping, loving, adoring   Eila.

"*P.S.*—If you decide on coming straight on here, would you mind bringing for me, from Paris, one dozen pair of gloves—three buttons—$6\frac{1}{2}$? You can choose the colours you like best. The gloves here are *execrable*.   E. M."

There was much to surprise Bertrand in this letter — his uncle's reconciliation most of all. "The other," he said, bitterly, "follows as a matter of course." He paced the room in deep thought, paused, re-read the letter, and resumed his walk. "Can this be true about my uncle?" was his idea; "or is it another trick—another wheel within the wheel of her falsehood?" At last he was apparently satisfied that the statement as to his uncle must be true. "But," he said, tossing the letter from him, "if his fortune were a hundred times larger, and his favour a hundred times more valuable, and I could only have them on this condition, I would say, 'Never.' I must answer this letter, I suppose; and I must write to Sir Roland and Mr M'Killop. These letters will require thought. I can't begin to-night, though; I shall be having the fever back. This business seems to have taken it out of me a good deal. I feel as tired as if I had walked a hundred miles. I'll go to bed. No; perhaps I had better sit up and see Pigott. I ought to have told him about my affairs before. He has been awfully kind. I'll tell him to-night, and take his advice as to the tone of my letters. When it comes to be a matter of hard common-sense, his advice is worth having." Then he threw himself upon the sofa, much exhausted, and waited for his friend. As his friend was returning from his party, he chuckled to himself on this wise—" Well, I've got a lead for him at last that he can't help following. It's perfectly childish of him, all this mystery; bad for him too. He's too strong now to be damaged by the excitement; and when it's over, he'll be all the better for it. I'll have it out with him to-night;" with which determination he joined his friend.

" Sleeping, Bertrand?" he cried, cheerily, as he entered the room.

" No, no; I was only resting a bit."

" Well, you must waken up, and hear all about my dissipation. After our quiet life, I feel like a young lady just come home from her first ball, and I must talk it all over."

" How is the widow?"

" The excellent person you allude to is not on the war-path. Her gallant husband still slakes his thirst in salubrious Bundlecund."

" How did you find that out?"

" I circumvented it by degrees — drew the conversation to the Indian regimental funds, in connection with which, a man is described in the matrimonial language of the East as good for so much, 'dead or alive;' and I saw that Curtis's posthumous advantages were still in prospect."

"And had you a lot of people there?"

"Ten or twelve—and a good enough dinner. A brother—M'Kascal—did host—a man rather of the Tainsh pattern, but stupider. He had a deplorable story about a capercailzie ; nobody would listen to it, but somehow it seemed to entangle itself with the conversation, and kept rising at the most unlooked-for times, all through dinner. Then there was an old fogy — also Scotch, and very fierce and argumentative. I suppose he thought I looked like a Tory, for he kept dangling little controversial baits in front of me, in a Radical sense. He abused the Army Estimates, and was awfully sold when I agreed with him ; he pronounced Gladstone to be a 'Phœnix,' when I agreed with him again, on the ground that he was for ever rising on the ashes of his old principles. He didn't quite seem to understand the allusion, but, considering it hostile, kept reiterating the statement that, 'say what they liked, he was a " Phœnix," and a " Phœnix " he would prove himself.' The whole thing got rather into a cross-purpose jumble at one time, for M'Kascal was a Tory, and stuck by his principles, without, however, relinquishing his yarn : so that at one time it appeared that, if people only stuck to the capercailzie, Ireland would be pacified ; whereas if Gladstone happened to be sitting upon eggs, and you came upon him in a wood, the chances were ten to one he would come at you like a steam-engine. The Phœnix and the capercailzie were really distracting. But lovely woman was there to mollify everything — M'Kascal's wife and the Phœnix - man's daughter ; the former talked about something she called ' protoplasm.' It seems to be a new sort of arrowroot, which does not necessarily, as she assured me, impeach the veracity of Holy Writ. She seemed perfectly sober too, so I suppose that confounded capercailzie has been too much for her intellect. It would pretty soon do for mine, I know. The younger lady was very arch,—told me she knew *all* about me and my friend up yonder (you); and wasn't it odd and mysterious ? I admitted that it was, but how ? Ah ! there it was — couldn't I guess ? No, I couldn't. How stupid I was ! was it true that officers were all stupid and conceited ? Yes, I believed so. Ah ! there I was — fishing for compliments ! but I must guess, guess. Well, perhaps she had read about us in the Bournemouth Visitors' List? No, she hadn't—a very, very dear friend of hers had told her about us. A lady? Yes, and *such* a nice girl. Unnecessary to say so of a 'very, very dear friend' of hers.

"There I was, again, with my absurdity. How did *I* know *she* was not horrid and nasty, and therefore the friend of horrid and nasty girls? I quite felt the justice of the question, and said I gave up the riddle. 'Well,' she said, 'you must have patience; she is coming in here this evening. You shall have a surprise. I *quite* look forward to seeing your meeting. It's almost romantic, I declare. I wouldn't for worlds miss the meeting. Certainly I won't tell you who she is.' And she didn't, but gushed and prattled away on other subjects ; and what with her archness, and the protoplasm, and the capercailzie, and the Phœnix, and the Aberdonian clangour of the voices all round the table, I can assure you I was not sorry when dinner was over. When we got to the drawing-room, who do you think the mysterious lady proved to be? Not that you'll guess any more than I did. I was glad to see her, however—although I can't say there was much romance about the meeting. She was always rather a friend of mine ; but, by the by, Bertrand, you've become such a dark horse, I don't know whether she is a friend of yours any longer. Perhaps" (with mock gravity) " I had better change the subject ? "

" Not at all : you may talk of any man, woman, or child under the sun, I assure you."

" Very well, I will.   It was Morna Grant."

" Morna Grant here ! "

" In the flesh ; and apparently in better spirits than the last time we saw her."

" What is she doing here ? "

" Abiding, residing with some of her mother's ancestors, I should say, from the name, which begins with a sneeze, turns into a cough, and ends airily in a hiccup.   I won't attempt it."

" Don't, please.   I certainly should not have expected to meet her here."

" She asked very kindly for you."

" Hum ! "

" Hoped she would see you."

" Ah ! "

" Gave me her address, that we might call."

" Oh ! "

" What a genius you have for monosyllables

to-night! I told her about your illness. She had only just heard of it. Wasn't that odd?"

"No; why should she have heard of it?"

"Ah! why indeed, of course? And then she said——but, hang it! perhaps you'll blaze out, and think me impertinent if I say what she said!"

"Not I; go on."

"Well, of course, Bertrand, I know nothing of your affairs. I have only conjectured; and, after all, it seems, from what she says, that my conjectures have not been correct."

"As how?"

"Well, not to mince matters, she began to talk about her people, and your—your engagement, you know, and that it had been suspended for a time, but that it was all on again, and the marriage to come off immediately. I said I knew nothing about it; but you hadn't been corresponding with her people—I knew *that*—and that I thought you would have told me if the marriage was coming off. I said I thought she must be mistaken. But she said that was impossible, for she had had a letter from her people —her mother or her step-sister, I forget which —this very evening, announcing that the marriage is to take place at Pau a few weeks after this."

"Ha! ha!" laughed Bertrand.

"I must say, Bertrand, I think you might have told an old pal like me. Here have I been cherishing a spirit of malice and all uncharitableness against the future Mrs Cameron. Why on earth didn't you tell me you were going to be married?"

"Why didn't I tell you? because it's an infernal lie from beginning to end."

"Odd, that; for I should have said that if truth were possible in a woman—I don't assert it is, mind—probably it might be possible in Morna Grant."

"Granted, granted; I have no doubt she believed what she told you. She was deceived—lied to—that's all; don't you see?"

"No, hang me if I do. It's as mysterious as the proto—what d'ye call it? I'll have a pipe; and you had better go to bed—you are looking done up."

"No, no; I wish to talk to you, Pigott. I have a lot to say to you on this very subject. I was going to speak to you about it to-night at any rate. I daresay you've been surprised that

I have never alluded to my engagement since I came back?"

"My dear fellow, you ought to know by this time, that nothing ever surprises me."

"No matter; I ought to have spoken to you about it before. I owed it to you, Pigott. You've been kinder to me than I ever dreamt it possible a man could be. I've never thanked you; but I've felt it, old fellow—believe me, I have. Very few men would have gone through what you have for me, and——"

"There, there, Bertrand. For heaven's sake don't gush about it! I hate that sort of thing, you know. If it hadn't amused me to nurse you, I wouldn't have done it, be sure of that. Now, go on with your yarn."

"Well, if you won't be thanked, you shan't be. Pigott, you were right about—about Miss M'Killop."

"I never said anything about her."

"Not in words—even in words you hinted things that made me angry,—but I knew by your manner you didn't believe in her: was I not right?"

"Well, if you put it to me, frankly, I never did, from the moment I clapped eyes on her.

If you would like to throw things at me, say so, and I'll go to bed."

"No; it's all over between us long ago. I am not going to indulge you with a tirade against her, and female faithlessness, and all that sort of thing, however."

"*Soit pour dit*, by all manner of means."

"I will simply tell you that she treated me— that she treated me very ill, and that she was actually guilty of falsehood."

"Ha! ha! ha!—I beg your pardon, Bertrand, but your earnestness was so appalling; and then only to hear, after all, that the world goes round!"

"It may amuse you, but it very nearly killed me. I haven't the advantage of being a sceptic or a cynic—not even yet, you see."

"I sincerely beg your pardon, Bertrand. Upon my honour, I'm sorry I spoke as I did. The whole affair must have been hard on you, or you wouldn't have suffered as I have seen you suffer. Go on, old fellow; I won't transgress again."

And Bertrand went on and narrated all the particulars of his eventful visit to Edinburgh, and read him the letter just received—all without passion or comment of any description ; insomuch that Pigott said to himself, "What a boon that fever has been to him ! it has positively almost made him sensible." He dwelt pretty strongly upon his interview with old M‘Killop—fully exonerating him of complicity, as indeed the result—the unexpected compliance of Sir Roland—clearly did. It was rather a disappointment to Pigott to admit this, and also that the conviction of felony must have been satisfactorily explained. " It remains, however, a wonderful puzzle," he said, " how M‘Killop could have persuaded your uncle—not so much of his innocence, but to recognise its value in a convicted man. Even to tolerably unworldly people, the conviction would be worse than the guilt. Perhaps your uncle is thoroughly unworldly, however ? "

" On the contrary, perhaps there is not a more worldly man in existence."

" Then either M‘Killop must be one of the cleverest fellows out, or this letter is another specimen of his daughter's talent for fiction."

" I thought of that, but it is impossible ; it would be quite meaningless, for one thing : besides, detection would be so certain. No ; strange as it may sound, M‘Killop must have carried his point with Sir Roland.”

“Then, Bertrand, you’ve made about as narrow an escape as man ever did.”

“I have; and learned a lot of lessons into the bargain.”

“I fancy you rather agree with me about the fair sex now?”

“If you mean that I include them all in one common sneer, you are quite mistaken. You brag about your stern logic; mine may not be so stern, but I think it is fully more correct. It certainly doesn’t teach me to reason from one particular instance up to a general truth.”

“Spoken like a schoolman!”

“It is all very well to laugh, but yours is the absurdity; I think he would be a mean, miserable, petty creature who took to misanthropy or misogyny—or whatever the word is—for such a cause. It would be just as reasonable, if, after you had picked one sour apple in an orchard, you were to cry out, “Have nothing to do with that orchard; its apples are all sour!”

“You stick to your apples and I’ll cling to the ‘mahogany;’ but really you ought to sell out and go to the bar.”

"And as for unhappiness setting one against all creation, on the contrary, it ought to make one better and kinder."

"You must relinquish the idea of the bar, and declare for the Church; but wait till the bishop has said, 'Go forth and preach'—for the present, don't do it, like a good fellow. Why didn't you write to M'Killop at once, from Edinburgh?"

"I was nearly out of my mind at first; then you know I was ill; and then, afterwards, I thought silence was best. I fancied the young lady would take her own way of telling her father; and she must have been deceiving him all along."

"Evidently; how she has out-manœuvred herself! Fancy the row she'll get into with her own people!"

"That depends on how I answer her letter, and how I write to them. If I leave her to make her own story, no doubt she'll get out of it cleverly enough."

"Yes, and the next act in the piece will be a breach-of-promise case instituted by the unconscious M'Killop, and perhaps a second disinheritance by his amiable Excellency; — that would be quite in keeping with your old style. *Place aux dames* in all things, even if they should wish to walk into our reputations and our fortunes without an equivalent!"

"No, no, I would not consider myself bound to make any sacrifice for her; still, unnecessary cruelty is not in my line. We must talk this matter over seriously, however, before I write. To-night I am too tired; I must go to bed. And, of course, I must see Miss Grant to-morrow, for it will not do to have her publishing this fiction all over the place."

CHAPTER XXXIII.

We must leave our friends in Bournemouth for a little, and turn back some space in time, to trace the adventures of the M'Killop family since we last saw them—the day after the military ball in Edinburgh. They did not remain in the northern capital more than a week or two after that event. M'Killop stuck to the programme he had indicated to Bertrand, and took his family to Pau, where Sir Roland had announced his intention of passing the spring months, on his return from his colony.

Mrs M'Killop was not averse to this arrangement. Edinburgh was not altogether to her mind. Society did not open its arms to her as she had expected. By dint of elaborate dinners, and asking right and left, she managed, indeed, to get about her a certain set of people who were willing enough to go anywhere for a dinner, but

whose presence at her board shed no lustre there-
upon.   They were not the people she wanted, by
any means.   Her battered, semi - mythical old
pedigree was a drug in the Edinburgh market,
and her wealth was an object of suspicion, and
perhaps of some other feeling, in that not very
opulent city.   She could not get on, in fact, and
early became convinced that to sit all night long
at public balls alone and supperless, amid a
crowd of acid dowagers who would none of her,
for all her diamonds, while her step - daughter
danced and flirted, was a game that was decidedly not worth the candle.

Therefore M'Killop's suggestion, that they
should go abroad, was grateful to her.   She had
never been out of Scotland, but she felt that to
be on the Continent, at this time of year, was
highly *comme il faut*, and that opportunities of
making " nice friends " were not among the least
of the advantages to accrue from a residence in
some pleasant Continental town, where, she understood, the English visitors, even of the highest
distinction, fraternised without any " stiffness,"
and " liked you for your own sake," which the
Edinburgh Goths could not, in her case, be
induced to do, either for that or any other con-

sideration.   So she gladly shook the snow off her feet against the Modern Athens, and departed rejoicing for pastures new.   The plan did not suit Eila at all.   She was getting on very well in Edinburgh.   An occasional glimpse of her step-dame's sulky countenance, solitary in the bank of chaperones, rather added a zest to the pleasures of a ball; and she had several promising things in hand, some one of which, time might develop into a golden certainty.   She shone among the military.   Many artless youths of the profession glared on each other with hot eyes for her sake, and dreamed champagny dreams of matrimony and bliss on 5s. 3d. per diem; and although men more amply provided, and therefore of a greater *retenue*, curiously scrutinised Mrs M'Killop's florid equipments, and pondered whether bliss would not be rather heavily handicapped with a mother-in-law of *that* pattern, still such ponder-ings end generally in declaring for the match, handicap and all.

So here Eila was enjoying a triumph and play-ing a good game; whereas at Pau,—mindful of her guilty secret, she shuddered as she thought how the cards might run for her there. Sanguine she might be, but there was always a doubt, and *such* a doubt. She had to go, however—her feeble insinuation that it was almost indelicate to hunt Sir Roland as they were about to do, making no impression on her parents. So she went; and among the troops in and about Edinburgh, there was weeping, and wailing, and gnashing of teeth. She had an undeniable genius for making fools of men, even where nature had not anticipated her.

Mr M'Killop was very liberal in money matters, and, provided he was not bothered about the making of domestic arrangements, had no objection to pay for them in the most docile spirit. His wife had a sort of *carte blanche*, and as she had determined to make a sensation at Pau, she used the privilege boldly, and, it need scarcely be added, with the desired result.

They were soon lodged in the most elegant, and even gorgeous, *appartement* which money could procure, close to the Place Royale, on the noble terrace overhanging the river. No situation could be more picturesque—perhaps it is one of the finest points of view in the world; with its foreground of dashing river, and gently-sloping uplands, bosky with vineyards and dotted with graceful hamlets; and beyond, the great sweep of the Pyrenees, a mighty snow-clad phalanx, indescribable in their weird, wild majesty. No situation can be more picturesque; but it had higher attractions still for Mrs M'Killop—it was the most fashionable locality she could select in all the town.

She admired the Pic du Midi of course (though constantly asserting its inferiority to Ben Lomond), and the river below was very nice, and the adjacent chateau of Henri Quatre most satisfactory; but she looked upon all these things— the view, the *entourage*, &c.—much as she did upon the gilding, the ormolu, the velvet and the satin which made splendid the interior of her abode; she classed them all together as good things which she had hired for the season, to promote her personal splendour and social distinction, and for which she was paying a stiffish consideration.

A fine mountain? Yes, rather; but small blame to him—he cost her several extra napoleons per mensem. It was not Mrs M'Killop's mission at Pau, she felt, to stare at a snowy range; she could do that gratis at home, more days of the year than she cared for: nor yet to poetise over the birthplace of the gallant Henri;

Edinburgh Castle was twice as big, and was it not the birthplace of several royal Jamies? No, she was there to do what she could not do at home; and "monstrari," not "monstrare, digito" was to be her motto. The M'Killop equipage was magnificent; the liveries florid; the horses English, of purest blood and loftiest action; heraldic devices defied the laws of heraldry on every available panel, button, and strap of the harness; and, to crown all, Angus M'Erracher, in the bravery of his mountain plumage, acted the combined parts of *chasseur* and minstrel—now dancing attendance on his lady in the promenade, now scarifying the cars of the vicinity with the terrible utterances of his bagpipes. As to the lady's personal adornments, they were in keeping with all the other externals. In ancient love-songs the enamoured swain frequently undertakes to scour the world in search of ornaments worthy of Belinda's charms—to ransack the earth and harry the sea, and glorify her beautiful person with the results. Mrs M'Killop's appearance suggested the idea that somebody had actually been and gone and done all this. The well-bred English, of whom there was a fair sprinkling in the place, half forgot the conventional lack-lustre gaze, and muttered incisive little remarks to one another, as the tremendous equipage went flaunting past. The third - raters, who were in a vast majority, fell down and worshipped the golden calf. Americans, filled with envious admiration by the costliness of the spectacle, were reminded of the superior though somewhat similar " boil-up" of Mrs Thaddeus G. Cass of Boston, U.S.; and all the other nationalities *caramba'd*, and *sacré'd*, and *ecco'd*, as the delighted lady bowled about the town, sowing her cards broadcast, and overlooking no house which she believed to be the abode of an eligible. The Continental etiquette which gives the privilege of initiating social relations to the latest comer, delighted her, and she made the most of it. The visitor's list and the resident's list were mastered by her in one day, and, in three more, it was a very exceptional household which was not supplied with a large oblong ticket, gilt as to its edges, crested in a merry colour, and inscribed in big German letters—

Mrs M'Killop,
Of Tolmie-Donnochie.

The purchase of Tolmic-Donnochie was not yet a *fait accompli*, but a territorial title was not to be discarded on any such insufficient grounds.

From the Maire to the Prefet — from Mrs Dickinson-Tomkinson of the Lindens, Putney, to the Dowager Duchess of Esil—there were few exemptions. Mrs M'Killop shot her bolts and waited for the result. Not long. Her progress through the town had done its work well, and gossip and rumour were at work upon the new arrivals, without a moment's delay. The wildest contradictions circled about the coteries ; and Proteus himself could not have assumed a greater variety of characters than were assigned to the unconscious M'Killop.

He was a Scot who had naturalised himself in Russia, and made a colossal fortune ; he had married a Begum, and given Rachel a lac of rupees to Europeanise her complexion ; he was the proprietor of the Hebrides ; he owned a silver mine in Peru ; he had rigged the cotton market ; he had plundered the Viceroy of Egypt ; he had "contracted" for everything everywhere ; —in short, his wealth was the only point on which there was a shadow of unanimity ; but that was enough. Life is short everywhere ; and at Pau, where half the visitors are moribund, the reflection is laid to heart, and the motto there seems to be, " Let us eat, drink, and be merry, for to-morrow we die."

In the race with Death there is no time to be fastidious—no time to be wasted in preliminary inquiries as to the antecedents of those who can minister to the pleasures of the fleeting moment. So Mrs M'Killop's bolts were shot, and in a vast number of instances they reached the mark she had aimed at.

Of course there were cases of failure ; as with the Dowager Duchess, for instance, who, after curiously scrutinising Mrs M'Killop's wonderful card through her glass, promptly rang the bell, and ordered it to be taken forth of the premises and burned with fire ; or with her friend the Comtesse de Sac-à-papier, who exclaimed to her the same evening, " My God ! figure to yourself, my dear Duchess, that the great red turkey comes from paying her respects at me !" But these were exceptional cases, and bushels of cards speedily cumbered the drawing-room table of the new arrivals. The quantity was undeniable, whatever the quality may have been. Yet many of

the cards were inscribed with double surnames,—
to Mrs M'Killop an infallible sign of high distinction;—and as for the " castellated Irish"
who returned her visit, their name was legion.
What would she have ?   In a week they were
in the vortex of everything; balls by the half-
dozen every evening; picnics, riding - parties,
dinners, and all the rest of it.   Mrs M'Killop
was in the seventh heaven. Eila at once assumed,
beyond all dispute, the position of the sovereign
belle.   Her beauty was sufficient for that ; but
such beauty, backed by mines in Peru, and other
similar advantages, turned admiration into a
furore.   In a ball-room there was no getting
near her.   Men waited, two deep, to petition for
a dance ; and the *comitans caterva* of adven-
turers who swarmed about her as she rode out,
reached the dimensions of a squadron of cavalry.
A strange Bashi - bazouk squadron, too.   The
ever-mysterious Count, the gentleman from Ireland, the solemn Spaniard, and the full-blown
cap-à-pie tiger from third-rate London clubs,
trotted fiercely together, a solid phalanx ; while
fervid Yankees and airy French officers curveted
and titupped about, watching for a break in the
serried ranks.   From morning to night her life

was a perpetual triumph; the fatigue would have prostrated most girls in a week, but at the end of a fortnight Eila was as blooming as ever. She throve on homage and excitement, which certainly constitute a pleasant diet.

Poor old M'Killop all this time led a sufficiently quiet life. The object for which he had come there was very different. He had nothing to do with the orgies of the place. He was waiting, with a feverish impatience, for the arrival of Sir Roland, who was due by this time, and, absorbed in thoughts of the coming interview, took little heed of what went on about him. A solitary walk in the forenoon, a few hours of the newspapers in the English club, and a solitary evening at home—such was his programme. He resisted a thousand efforts at fraternisation, and his unsociability having to be accounted for, continued to make him the object of much speculation. He was revolving the pros and cons of a loan to the Sultan; he was meditating some gigantic scheme for swindling the public in an international sense; he had murdered some one in Mexico, and was a prey to remorse. Such and suchlike were the theories about him, as he unconsciously mooned about the place.

When his people happened to be at home, which was very seldom, he was more than ordinarily silent with them. A remark on the weather, or the non-arrival of Sir Roland, pretty nearly exhausted his communications for the day.

They had been at Pau for a good many weeks, and thus occupied, when a ball came off of more than usual distinction and splendour. It was given by people who occupied about the best position in the social orbit in which the M‘Killops moved, and was attended by many who belonged to a circle into which they had never penetrated. It had been a good deal looked forward to by them in consequence, and even more than usual pains were taken to give distinction to the toilette of "the Western Star," the *sobriquet* which, as humouring the theories of Peru and the Hebrides, the public had agreed to bestow on Eila.

She and her mother found that there were many people there with whom they were unacquainted, and the former noted with exultation, that the effect produced upon them by her appearance was all that could be desired. It was not merely admiration, it was surprise also. Most of them, of course, had seen her in the morning, when riding or driving, but she was perfectly aware that in the dress of the evening her charms were enhanced a hundred-fold. That "no one knew what she was" in fact, she would say, till they had seen her in this costume. To-night nothing could be more becoming than her dress, and she was in her very best looks. Her entrance created something like a sensation.

"Here comes our belle," said the lady of the house. "I must really introduce you to her at once."

The gentleman she addressed was an elderly man, certainly not of prepossessing, or even distinguished, appearance, though something in the hostess's manner towards him gave bystanders an idea that he was a person of distinction, in her opinion at all events. He was a man of the middle size, with a reddish face closely shaved, and sparse white hair carefully brushed to conceal baldness; his nose aquiline, but large and coarse; his mouth full and coarse, his under lip pendulous, his chin doubling, his eyes small and of a pale blue, set very close together. It was a nasty face, cunning and sensual. Notwithstanding these disadvantages, or rather, perhaps, to counteract them, he had all the appearance of paying much attention to his dress; and the alacrity with which he acquiesced in the introduction to Eila, and the satyr-like gaze which he fixed upon her from the moment of her entry, showed that he was not insensible, in some way or other, to female charms.

"Do so, pray," he said, in answer to the lady. "She is really lovely—lovely; her name is?"

"Miss M'Killop."

"Scotch, I suppose?"

"I think not. Mexican or Peruvian, or something," said the lady, confounding the girl's origin with that of her reputed wealth. "So charmed to see you, my dear Miss M'Killop! what a heavenly dress! and yourself more angelic, if possible, than usual." Then turning to the Satyr, who was basilisking the young beauty with his unholy blue eyes, "Let me present to you Sir ——." Here the music struck up with a tremendous fanfarade, close beside them, so that Eila did not catch the name. The handle, however, reached her, and she was civil, notwithstanding Sir ——'s age and unprepossessing appearance.

"Will you take pity upon the latest arrival in

Pau, Miss M'Killop?" he said, in a soft and harmonious voice; "a man without friends or acquaintance in the place, except our hostess, and dance a quadrille with me?"

"With pleasure; when shall it be?"

"Now, if you will, for you have made no engagements yet."

"How do you know that?" she asked, with a laugh.

"Because I was watching your triumphant progress from the moment you entered, and you were cruelly indifferent, and would not notice some score or two of aspirants."

The old gentleman was *très bien* after all, Eila thought, and she consented to dance the first quadrille with him—a complaisance which sent some half-a-dozen Bashi-bazouks to the right about, gnawing their hearts.

"You know all the world here, Miss M'Killop, of course," said her partner; "please enlighten my darkness, and tell me who are your lions."

"I really don't think we have any to boast of here; there's Baron Brovaski, over there; I believe he would be hanged or knouted if he went home, which makes him a sort of lion, I suppose."

"He reverses the proverb, and thinks it better to be a living lion than a dead ass, I suppose : and who is that lady, rather old, in green satin with diamonds ?"

"That," said Eila, with some awe, as mentioning the marchioness of the place, "is Lady Grampington."

"Indeed! how very odd I should not recognise her! one of my oldest friends. I've been long abroad, though, and time passes. Dear, dear, how time does pass!" and something like a sigh escaped from his lips; and Eila looked at him with a little semi-pathetic glance of sympathy. Was he not Sir Blank Blank himself, and the very dear friend of the Marchioness of Grampington ?"

"Time is a sad dog," he continued ; "I was a boy yesterday, and look at me now.'

Eila complied with the request ; but although the leering eyes invited her to say something as to exceptions occasionally made by "the sad dog," she only smiled.

"But it does not signify what Time does with us. Ah! dear me, no, that is nothing. It is what he dares to do to beautiful forms — beautiful forms that are so beautiful as to make fools even of old fogies like myself, and for a little make us forget that we are no longer young. To-night, for instance, what business have I to be dancing with you?"

"What, indeed?" thought Eila; but she replied that she was afraid he was getting tired of her already, and wanted an excuse to be off to the Marchioness, adding, "Perhaps she was an old flame?"

"No, she wasn't; but I can remember her as Lucy Grey, a very pretty girl; and perhaps she would tell you she remembers me as a—no matter what—what you can't conceive now, I'm sure," with an amorous twinkle.

"The old goose is fishing for compliments," thought Eila—"I'll give him one;" and went on,—"When you are really an old man you may take the privilege of age; at present, you have no business to ask me whether I think you handsome. I am not going to tell you, at all events."

Her partner was enchanted. "I believe I am almost old enough to be your grandfather," he replied.

"Not almost, but altogether," she thought, as she answered, "Even that needn't make you very old."

“No, true ; you are as young as Aurora, and” (in a tender voice) “far more cruelly bewitching.”

“I must really send you to the Marchioness,” said Eila, using her eyes, partly for practice’ sake, with all her might and main. “If you *will* play at being an old man, you must play with elderly females. How long are you going to stay here ?”

“I hadn’t thought of it till to-night, and now I can’t answer it except by a return question, ‘How long are you ?’ ”

“Really,” said Eila, blazing away with her eyes till the frosty blue of her partner’s thawed and watered, and his eyelids blinked five hundred to the minute, “you are too silly ; well, if you must know, I think we shall stay till the end of the season.”

“I may warn the hotel, then, that my apartments will be required till the end of the season ?”

“What nonsense you talk ! What can it matter to you whether we stay here or not ?”

“Because—well, let it be unsaid—will you patronise me if I stay? May I come and see you ?”

"Of course you may, if you like."

"To-morrow?"

Eila laughed merrily. "If you please, but you will tire of me all the sooner, I assure you. There's the dance over; run away to the Marchioness. Adieu."

"Give me another dance to-night?"

"Impossible; look at these," and she pointed to the Bashi-bazouks yearning all around her.

"It is despair for me, then, till to-morrow."

"Stay; you may take me to supper, if you like, by-and-by."

"I count the moments till supper-time. *Au revoir;*" and with a profound reverence and a Pandean grimace, he went off to his noble friend.

Eila was much amused and gratified; it was a new sensation, flirting with a sexagenarian. She said to herself that she was inexorable and resistless; that age and experience, youth and innocence, fell before her indiscriminately, as the bearded grain and the intervening flowerets fall before the sickle of the reaper. It was great fun; and she told the flowerets of the *grand vieux milor Anglais*, and his carryings-on, and wasn't it amusing? but the Bashi-bazouks did not quite seem to see *that*. And her venerable swain came back to her at supper-time, and took her down, and over the champagne his tenderness became yet more demonstrative, and Eila played him like a salmon, till his eyes glittered, and his pendulous lip hung down like a turkey's jowler, and he vowed he must call the next day; and might he? and she said " Yes;" and he squeezed her hand at parting, and kept his promise about calling; for next forenoon, while she and her father were sitting in the drawing-room, the door was thrown open and he marched in, the servant announcing " Sir Roland Cameron ! "

It chanced that Mr M‘Killop was in a more sociable humour than usual this morning, and (his wife being still in bed) was chatting with his daughter, or rather listening to her as she rattled off a sort of *précis* of the last few days' doings. She was full of the previous night's ball; and having visions of using Sir —— somehow or other, *viâ* the Marchioness even, perhaps —as a means of getting into a better and more exclusive set—she dwelt a good deal, both in thought and word, upon him and his kindness (for she called it "kindness" to her papa).

" He actually insists upon calling to see me," she said.

" Considering your circumstances, Eila, I don't think——but you say he is an old man ? "

" Oh yes—as old as the Pic du Midi."

" I forgot what you said his name was ? "

" I can't tell you—Sir Somebody Something ;" and, almost at this moment, the servant's announcement supplied the required intelligence.

Sir Roland ambled into the room, dressed for conquest, and, as need hardly be said of one who accused himself so frequently of age, in the most youthful of toilettes, his eyes almost invisible from the benign rapidity with which his eyelids blinked, and his baggy lips pursed into a corresponding smile.

The sudden entrance of a bomb-shell through the roof, is a favourite figure of speech for measuring surprise and consternation, but anything of the sort would have been tame and commonplace to Mr and Miss M'Killop compared with the entrance of their visitor. Eila turned pale as death ; and as for old M'Killop, he looked as stunned and stupid as if a butcher had been practising knock-down blows on his head for the previous five minutes. He had hardly time to feel double surprise at the affectionate manner of his visitor's entrance, before Eila recovered herself with an effort, and, welcoming Sir Roland, introduced him to her father as " the gentleman she had been telling him of, as her partner of the previous evening." She was determined the *éclaircissement* should not come off, in *her* presence, at all events. M‘Killop rose mechanically, and made a sort of shambling bow without lifting his eyes, and then reseated himself, in a state of perfect mental darkness.

For the last few months he had been looking forward to an interview with this man now before him. His mind had dwelt upon the subject almost to the exclusion of every other. In imagination he had rehearsed his conduct at the interview a hundred times. A hundred times he had paraded the line of arguments he meant to employ, and the reserve which, in case of their failure, he held in readiness, and, so to speak, mobilised. As for preambles and prefatory speeches, he had them cut and dried by the dozen, all ready for selection, when the hour came and the man. Such imaginary rehearsals, however, involve some preconception of the person who is to be addressed. Of course Mr M‘Killop had formed one of Sir Roland ; but Rhadamanthus was not more unlike Silenus than was the tall and upright figure, the stern and statesmanlike appearance, of Mr M'Killop's pre-conception, unlike the leering reality now before him. So the shock was in a manner double; for not only was the mode of the meeting a total violation of the programme, but the man met seemed to be a sort of person for whom an entirely new set of tactics must be devised. The sudden appearance of Sir Roland thus produced the effect of chaos in Mr M'Killop's mind, the result of which was, that Sir Roland remained for the present unconscious that he was visiting his would - be relatives. The effect which his entrance produced was by no means lost upon that gentleman, and he glanced quickly from the pale face and fluttering demeanour of Eila, to the vacant consternation written in her father's face, and he was baffled. He had a large experience both of men and women, and, in a career of not altogether blameless gallantries, he had often found it expedient to trace the progress of his affairs in the faces of the former as well as of the latter. But his vanity could not possibly supply an explanation for Eila's agitation, and his conscience for once was unable to account for that of her father. He was not the man, how-

ever, to waste time in fruitless speculation; so
he sat down and gaily devoted himself to the
young lady, after favouring her parent with a
single glance of slight curiosity.

Eila had a difficult part to play. The supreme object of the moment with her, always
was to fascinate him who was with her for the
moment. It was clearly consistent with her
duty, as well as with her inclination, to fascinate
at present; but there are different forms of
fascination, and the question was, whether it was
in the capacity of her future husband's uncle
that he was to be charmed, or in that of an
admirer on his own account. It was a nice
point, but her own instinct told her that, with
this man, the latter was the alternative to adopt;
and the resolution taken, she let her eyes hold
the position with their full battery, till she had
rallied her composure sufficiently to bring her
tongue into action with effect.

Sir Roland gave her as much time as was
necessary, and prattled away himself with airy
volubility. It had been a charming ball—his
first since his return to Europe—a delightful
revival after the antipodes; for, wasn't it odd?
he had just come from the antipodes; and she

was looking marvellous—simply marvellous; but late hours could leave no trace upon Aurora, though even Tithonus could not say he felt much the worse for wear this morning—he! he! he! hum!

And Aurora, puzzled, but on the chance that her *vis-à-vis* was supposed to be Tithonus, explained by her eyes that, in her opinion, that gentleman was in the highest state of repair.

" And the Marchioness, my dear Miss M‘Killop —shall I tell you about the Marchioness? and what she said to me?"

" Pray do, if it was not too tender."

" I think I must revenge myself by not telling you. You gave me a lecture against vanity last night, and it would not be right to minister to that of the lecturer."

" Oh! she spoke of me, did she?" cried Eila, with sparkling eyes.

" My dear young lady," replied Sir Roland, with a high shrug and expanded palms, " you are really too childish. Now, do you think that I *could* have stayed with the Marchioness for an instant if she had talked on any other subject? I put it to you."

" What did she say about me?" said Eila,

acknowledging the compliment with an appropriate *œillade.*

"What did she say?—the same story as is told you by every mirror—nay, by every eye—you look into,—*that*, as a matter of course, however. The refrain of whatever she said was simply this—'I *must* know that sweet angel. Sir Roland, do you hear? I must know her. Do you think she would care to know me? I declare I am in love with her.' I really hope," he added, with grave earnestness, "you will be civil to the Marchioness. She is a very dear creature, and an old friend of mine;" and Eila was satisfied that that afternoon her ladyship would appease the yearnings of her heart and call, and assured Sir Roland that she need expect nothing but civility at her hands. He was going to be useful, *ce cher parent;* and she had a Ruth-like feeling that his marchionesses should certainly be her marchionesses.

"You also accused me of vanity last night," he went on; "and, do you know, you have succeeded, after all, in making me vainer than I have been for years."

"How, pray?"

"Why, you had not forgotten the Methuselah

you danced with last night,—you had actually been talking of him,—now tell me how you described him?"

"Oh! no, no; that would never do. I also told you last night not to fish for compliments. You are sadly neglectful of my orders. What a pretty bouquet of violets! but you ought to wear something brighter. Let me substitute this rose," and she took one from the *jardinière* and offered it; and, with a profusion of fine speeches and amorous smiles, the flower was accepted, "but only as an exchange—I protest, only as an exchange. Make me perfectly happy, and accept the violets;" and, after a little coy demurring, the violets were accepted and stuck in Eila's bosom.

The clouds had been slowly rolling away from Mr M'Killop's bewildered mind, and he had become conscious of what was going on, but he was still incapable of speech or action, the tone of the conversation, in which he was altogether ignored, holding him in a minor trance of astonishment. When the flower episode took place, he relieved his feelings by a long-drawn breath —a sort of gasp, in fact, which sounded, through his asthmatic apparatus, like the snort of a very large seal just come above water.

"God bless me!" said Sir Roland, starting, and putting up his eye-glass; "anything wrong with Mr a—a— ?"

"No, no," said Eila, as her father said nothing; and then Sir Roland inquired archly by telegraph whether the snorter could not be induced to remove himself.

Eila shook her head warningly, and Sir Roland, feeling that a confidential understanding had been established between them by these signals, dropped his voice into a confidential tone, so as to be only partially audible to Mr M'Killop. In the language of "soft eyes and low replies" Eila responded, and the interview went on delightfully, but protracted itself to such a length that Mr M'Killop at last thoroughly recovered possession of his faculties, and, to Eila's consternation, his voice, harsh and grating as a saw, suddenly broke in upon their undertoned colloquy.

"I think you are the governor of ——, Sir Roland ?"

"Eh ? what ?" said Sir Roland, with a start.

M'Killop repeated his question.

"Yes," said Sir Roland, staring at him curiously through his glass — "yes;" and then to

Eila, "perhaps Mr a — a — a" (N.B. — The fiercest love made to a young lady does not the least imply that you remember her family name in any other member of the family)—perhaps Mr a—a—Mac—Mac—ah!—is interested in the colony."

"I declare," said Eila, rising, "I will not have business talked. I know what happens with papa when the colonies come on the *tapis*."

"Yes," said M'Killop, "I am much interested in the colony."

"Were you out there?" inquired Sir Roland.

"Never mind," replied Eila; "I forbid you to talk of it." Her agitation returned in spite of herself.

"And deeply interested in you, Sir Roland," continued M'Killop.

"Monstrous kind, I'm sure," said his Excellency, inquiring, by a slight gesture, of Eila, if her parent was not a little troubled with imbecility; and indeed his conduct throughout might warrant the suspicion.

"And I have a pressing desire to converse with you, Sir Roland," M'Killop went on.

"Very glad, I'm sure, to give you any information, but Miss M'Killop's orders are my law ; no colonial shop to be talked at present, eh ? Ha ! ha ! "

M'Killop, however, was not to be repressed. He rose and joined them ; and Eila, seeing that in another moment the murder would be out, rose hurriedly and said, " I see you are both burning to get to business, so I will run away. Good-bye, Sir Roland—so kind of you to call ! "

" Going ! this is too cruel ; no, no, not going ? " and he playfully skipped towards the door, as if to intercept her retreat.

" Really I am—I must indeed—good-bye."

" Ah ! when shall we meet, then ? " he murmured ; " do you ride to-day?—walk?—drive? Where shall I meet you, beautiful Aurora ? "

" I can't exactly tell, but we are sure to meet. Everybody meets everybody everywhere in Pau ; " and, with a parting glance of ineffable witchery, she tripped out of the room.

CHAPTER XXXIV.

MANY men have an entirely different set of manners for the two sexes, and Sir Roland was a strong instance of this. His natural manner with men was ungenial at best, and somewhat curt and insolent when he had no particular call to be otherwise—characteristics which officialism is not likely to improve. On this occasion he divested himself with surprising rapidity of all the amenities, and, when he turned from closing the door upon Eila, his manner very much expressed something like—" Now, my good fellow, it's not the least good boring me, so just cut it short, will you ? "

" Some infernal question about wool, or some wiseacre's suggestion about the emigrants, of course," he thought; " I won't be entrapped, though ; I won't stay. I'll give him two minutes," in pursuit of which determination he declined to sit down, and began to pull on his gloves as if to indicate that extreme brevity was desirable.

"We have heard of each other before, Sir Roland," began M'Killop, adopting the preface which came uppermost.

Sir Roland was not aware, but would not combat the proposition.

According to the programme, he should have investigated it; but he didn't, and M'Killop was at fault, for a moment.

" I know I am addressing a man of the world," he resumed.

Sir Roland bowed.

" And I believe of humanity ? "

Sir Roland stared.

" Knowledge of the world—experience of its sins, its sorrows, its temptations, ought to make us humane."

Sir Roland rapidly buttoned his coat.

Poor M'Killop was all abroad, jumbling his prefaces up together in the most hopeless manner, but his interlocutor would not help him, and he stumbled on.

"I am a father, Sir Roland."

" So it would appear, Mr Smith."

" And you are not."

Sir Roland was very glad to hear it.

"But you are an uncle."

"Yes, sir; and a cousin; and I have been a grandson, and a great-grandson, and a brother, and a nephew; and Abraham begat Isaac, and Isaac Jacob, and, good God! my good sir, if this is all you have to say, I'm very sorry I haven't time at present to listen. I thought you wanted to ask a question about the colony?" Sir Roland had formed a sudden suspicion that M'Killop was going to ask a favour for some relative, which made it expedient that his temper should appear violent.

"No, not about the colony," replied M'Killop. "I have the pleasure of knowing your Excellency's nephew, and——"

"And you wish to speak to me about him?" cried his Excellency, turning purple.

"I do, Sir Roland."

"Then let me tell you that I decline to speak about him; we have ceased to have any connection."

"Temporarily, I hope."

"Why the devil, sir, may I ask, should *you* hope so?"

"For many reasons. He is a very fine young man; I am much attached to him; and——"

“Quite enough, sir—quite enough. I fail to discover his merits. I think he is an ungrateful young hound, mad with folly and vanity, and with a taste for low society which I can neither share nor countenance. You may be aware of his last escapade—his matrimonial ambition?”

“I am, and that is the very subject I have to speak about—that is my supreme interest in him.”

“Indeed? Perhaps, from your colonial experience, you may know the fortunate criminal he wishes to make his father-in-law?”

Sir Roland desired to be impertinent, but nothing could have been more pertinent to M‘Killop’s wishes than the question.

“No one better, Sir Roland. I am the man himself.”

“Almighty heavens!” exclaimed Sir Roland, with slow emphasis on each word, sinking, from sheer astonishment, into a chair; “and that— then—is it possible that the young lady who has just left us——”

“Is his betrothed—and, I trust, his future wife.”

Sir Roland could only repeat his pious exclamation.

He sat in as stupid a state of mental eclipse as Mr M‘Killop had suffered under during the earlier part of the visit.

" Almighty heavens!"

It was now M‘Killop's turn to be fluent, and he was so,—fluent and earnest, pleading the cause of the young people—and himself.

He dwelt on the pecuniary advantages he offered, and on the merits of his daughter; the passionate affection of the young people for one another; his own retrieved character, his position as a man of wealth and landed property, and the unlikelihood that, under a new name and in such altered circumstances, he should be identified as the convict of forty years ago. The very marriage itself would almost secure that, he said.

This was his peroration, whereupon Sir Roland rose and said : " That is a strong argument from your point of view, no doubt. From mine, it is scarcely so telling. My name, in fact, is to cover your infamy. Upon my word, your assurance almost surprises me. I have seen a good deal of your class, but this I was scarcely prepared for. That you, a low, thieving gutter - blood should dare to speak to me—to *me*, of all men, in such terms! Hang me, if it isn't beyond human belief! No more of it, sir," and he turned to the door.

" One moment, Sir Roland," said M'Killop, and Sir Roland, who seemed half paralysed, stopped mechanically.

" It would be useless, I suppose, to urge upon you that I was wrongfully convicted—that I was innocent throughout—made the tool, though not the accomplice, of others; it would be useless, I suppose, to ask you to see the confirmation of this in my conduct as a convict—in my unblemished life afterwards—in my success, even."

" I should rather think it would, sir. I have no fine taste in romantic fiction, however melodramatic. Get some one to put the story on the stage. Your son-in-law-to-be is just my idea of a stage-hero; let him take up that line, and make his *début* in the piece. Your story is, no doubt, quite within the range of dramatic credibility; address it to the pit and the gallery; it won't stand daylight, and it won't do off the boards."

Again Sir Roland turned to go, and again M'Killop stopped him.

" You have used very injurious and uncalled-for expressions, Sir Roland, but I will not retaliate. You scout the idea of my innocence, and you decline the proposals made in my letter, without qualification. Be it so. We have exhausted fair means. I shall try another line with you. The marriage is a very great object to me, partly for the reason which you consider my paramount reason. I do not deny it; but also for another reason which *is* paramount. Sir Roland, I have it in my power to ruin you."

"Ha! ha!" laughed his Excellency; "well put in; the gallery at the Adelphi would taste that: and so you have it in your power to ruin me, have you? but you won't, if I give in to your proposal?"

"No, I won't."

"And how, pray, is my ruin to be effected?—through the reputation or the purse?"

It is just possible that Sir Roland was not so clear as to the impossibility of the former alternative, or he might not have cared to linger bandying words with a "thievish gutter-blood" on the subject. His manner was, however, quite calm again, and even bantering.

"I understand," replied M'Killop, "that your appointment has lapsed, or is about to lapse, and it is said that your employment again is unlikely.

That will leave you rather short of money from an official source, won't it ?"

" Supposing it to be as you say, do you propose to give me an equivalent income as the price of my compliance ?" sneered Sir Roland.

" On the contrary, I propose to deprive you of your private income also, and make you a beggar."

" A strong inducement to compliance, certainly. You are indeed most persuasive. Now really, my good man, a person at your time of life—and of prison experience, too—should be too sharp to attempt such a very stupid, rusty, old absurdity as that ; I must really leave you—you quite cease to interest me."

" As you will, but it will pay you better to stay and listen to me. Not only do I repeat that I have power to ruin you, but, by doing so, my daughter's marriage could come off with even more pecuniary advantage to her than with your compliance."

" And yet your affection for me is so great —your consideration for a praiseworthy public servant, &c. &c., so strong—that you hold your hand. For shame ! for shame !"

" Not at all ; I can't ruin you without putting myself in an uncomfortable position."

"That is a comfort for me : it is clear you won't ruin me, then."

" I will, if necessary.   I am quite frank, you see."

"Charmingly so ; but not quite so explicit as one might desire."

"I shall be perfectly explicit ; but to be so, I must trouble you to listen to a short story about myself."

" A most interesting subject, and no apology called for."

Sir Roland saw by the man's manner that there was *something*, after all, which it would be well for him to hear, in his own interests, and so he sat still and listened.

" Some forty years ago," M'Killop went on, " a young and simple-minded man was employed as a clerk in a lawyer's office in Edinburgh—not only employed, but trusted by his employers in many ways ; insomuch so that he had facility of access—but this was partly, indeed, from the carelessness of his employers—to the boxes in which their clients' papers, titles, securities, &c., were preserved.

"These boxes were frequently left unlocked, and the young clerk, from mere inquisitiveness, used occasionally to examine some of the quaint old deeds which they contained.

"This fact he accidentally suffered to escape him in a mixed company, when, in the course of an argument, he quoted from one of these documents, stating where and how he had been able to consult it.

"There was some banter as to his prying propensities at the moment; but, as he was innocent in thought and intent, he took little heed of it.

"Some one, however, who was present at the time, had reported to his employers that their papers were being overhauled, and their private business discussed publicly by their clerk; and the result was that he was summarily dismissed, thrown out of the chance even of employment, and reduced to the most miserable straits for a livelihood.

"He had been for some time in this state, when he met a person who had been present on the evening when he had compromised himself about the inspection of the papers. This person was civil and kind, affected not to have heard of his disgrace, sympathised with him when he had told the story, gave him some little pecuniary assistance, and told him to apply to him in future when in extreme necessity. The clerk's extreme necessities were very frequent, and he availed himself of the friendly permission pretty freely.

"At last, one day his benevolent friend told him that he was personally, and by his relatives, closely interested in a lawsuit then impending, which involved his and their loss or gain pecuniarily to a very large amount.

"The opposite party had got hold of documents (to his knowledge) which would clearly give the result, if in his (the speaker's) possession, in his favour. They denied possession of them, however, and were suppressing them unjustly and fraudulently. He had reason to believe that they were in the custody of the clerk's late employers, he said ; and was he cognisant of any papers docketed with the names of the parties interested ? The clerk had some notion that he had seen papers of the description, and certainly knew the box where they were likely to be, if in the custody of the firm. The gentleman was much interested at hearing all this, but said nothing more on the subject, at the moment.

"In a day or two after, however, the clerk was invited to come and have an interview with him, and then the gentleman, after enlarging on

the scandalous iniquity of which he was the victim by the suppression of these papers, asked the
clerk if, in his opinion, it would be morally wrong
were he (the speaker), under the circumstances,
to possess himself of them by stratagem ?   The
clerk was not sure, but he inclined to think that
stratagem would be morally admissible, under the
circumstances stated.

"'Then,' said the gentleman, 'you are the
only person who can save us.   You know the
premises ; you know the boxes ; you know the
careless habits of the firm, where keys are left
or hidden at night, &c. &c. ; and, in short, you
shall have five hundred pounds and a free passage
to America, if you hand me over these papers
to-morrow night.   It is only spoiling the Egyp-
tian at worst,' he said ; 'and when they discover
the loss, they will be unable to act, as they have
sworn that the papers are not in their possession.'

"The proposal was rather overwhelming at
first ; for, although it might be in the cause of
justice, it was undeniably a burglary that was
proposed.   The young man's circumstances, however, were desperate, the bribe was large, and
eventually he consented.

"That very night he effected an entrance into

his late employer's premises, and, after a short search, lighted upon a large quantity of papers with the looked-for docketing. He had no time to examine them, or anything else, narrowly; and as there were other detached papers in the same box, he thought it safer to take them all without investigation, and he did so. In leaving the premises he was detected by the porter of the establishment, and pursued ; but he escaped for the moment, and carried the papers in all haste to the gentleman who had employed him. Nothing could exceed this person's delight : 'but here,' he said, 'are some other papers I have nothing to do with, and I am not going to put myself within reach of the law ;—take them, and as you have been seen and probably recognised, let me recommend you to leave this town to-night, and the country as soon as you possibly can. Here is your reward in notes.' The clerk took the returned papers and thrust them into his pocket, went off in the greatest agitation to his lodging, changed his clothes, and disguised himself as much as possible, then packed up all his effects, and went to Leith, where he got a passage in a steamer to the Aberdeenshire coast. His parents and relatives, who were in humble life, lived in

that part of Scotland; and, bewildered and
almost instinctively—for his bewilderment and
his fears confused him—he went home to see
them once more before his departure, which was
now no longer optional, for America. This was
naturally a fatal step to take; and though he
reached his destination in safety, the day following, when he went into the neighbouring town
to make inquiries as to a passage across the
Atlantic, he was arrested, and taken back a
prisoner to Edinburgh.

"His parents heard of it, and fearing a search
(they were ignorant, illiterate people), and that
something to compromise him might be found in
his box, took the precaution of burying it. He
was tried, convicted, and transported. I was the
man, Sir Roland."

His Excellency signified by a gesture that he
quite understood so, and that he heartily con-
curred in the verdict.

"I had been long out of prison—long entirely
at freedom, I should say—and a rich and flourish-
ing man in the colony, when my parents, whom I
had been able to make comfortable for years,
died within a short time of each other. They
left no other children; and, having a real tender-

ness for them, I gave instructions that all their effects should be retained till my return to Scotland, of which I began to have a good prospect. Small articles, however, were to be sent out, for I wished to have something about me to remind me of the old folks. Among other things sent out was my own trunk, which had been buried, but dug up again after my transportation. My people had never opened it—the keys had been in my pocket when I was apprehended—and I suppose they had scruples about opening another man's box, even a son's, by forcing it. They were strict—very strict and scrupulous ; and my conviction might make them more so. Anyhow, the box had never been opened. I had forgotten all about its contents, and turned them over with little recollection or interest. At last I lighted on the coat I had worn on the night of the burglary, and in the pocket of it I found the bundle of documents which had been returned to me by the gentleman at whose instigation I had acted. Even the fact that these papers had ever been in my possession had passed from my recollection, and it was some time before I could recall the circumstances under which they were so. I had received them mechanically. I had been much agitated at the time, you must observe. I had just come from a most hazardous adventure : I had escaped capture very narrowly: I had received a sum of money that was large enough in my eyes to be the foundation of a fortune : and I had before me the necessity of expatriation and instant flight, not to mention the fear of detection. I don't think—I don't really believe—that any recollection of these papers was in my mind after I packed up the coat which contained them, on the night of their abstraction."

Sir Roland indicated by a faint groan that the question had no sort of interest for him, and was being discussed at unnecessary length.

" The discovery," M'Killop went on, " of these papers was a most unpleasant one to me ; and when I had examined them, and found that one at least was probably of vital importance, I was at a loss how to act. I must tell you that I had pled 'not guilty.' Morally I felt that I was not guilty, and even technically I was but very partially so. Whether the legal firm whose premises I had broken into were really, as my employer had said, afraid to charge me with the abstraction of papers which they had no right to possess, I do not know; certain it is that I was not charged with the theft of documents, but simply with burglariously entering certain premises, feloniously breaking open lockfast places, and abstracting some trumpery sum—I forget how much—in shillings, which, most likely, the porter who pursued me had appropriated to himself on his return, as a reward for his exertions. I had always maintained, as I always will, my inno-cence—morally——"

"Let us avoid morals, if *you* please, sir; I am not quite a fool," interpolated Sir Roland.

"I had always maintained it, I say, and to denounce myself now as in the possession of these papers, was to cut away the ground of success on which I stood from under my feet, and announce myself as guilty, where I really was not morally or intentionally guilty. If I had followed the dictates of the highest principle, however, I should, no doubt, have at once made public my discovery of these papers, but I hadn't strength of purpose to do it. I studied the documents very carefully, and took pains to inform myself of certain matters at home connected with them, and I came to the conclusion that, for the present at least, no one's interests suffered by my silence. An evil im-pulse once obeyed is apt to find ready obedience

on every after recurrence. In course of time an
interest came to be compromised by my silence,
and still I kept silence. I preserved the paper
until some future date.

" Your nephew was not born till after my discovery, Sir Roland."

" And what has that to do with it, pray ?"

" Only that one of the documents happens to
be a second will of your father's annulling his
previous disposition ; and, in case of your elder
brother having any children, withdrawing your
right to inherit the estate of Aberlorna in their
favour.

" Strictly speaking, Sir Roland, you·were entitled to enjoy Aberlorna for about eighteen
months, whereas you have now possessed it about
a quarter of a century."

" A forgery—a lie !" said Sir Roland ; " where
is this precious document ?"

" This precious document is in my possession.
Here it is ; satisfy yourself as to the signature,
and I will read you the contents." Sir Roland
carefully examined the document, without, however, receiving it into his own hands, and when
the text had been read aloud, M'Killop went on—
" The slightest reflection will show you that there

could be no object on my part to forge such a paper. My great desire has been to make restitution to your nephew of his rights—all along I have wished it; but I will not deny that I equally wished not to compromise myself by doing so. If I had declared the paper on its first discovery, by this time I should perhaps have been almost in as good a position as I am, but every day made it more difficult; and when I returned home and settled in Scotland to make a position, I began to despair of ever being able to set matters right in my own lifetime. An accident, however, threw your nephew in my way. I declare to you that such a solution as his marrying my daughter never occurred to me, till he came to ask me to sanction his engagement with her.

"Then I saw an opening to do him eventual justice, and also to make good to him, in so far as was possible, the loss he had sustained—all without compromising myself.

"If your sanction had been obtained, matters would thus have righted themselves in the natural course of events; but it was not so; and, on the contrary, I found myself for a second time, as it were, standing between him and his inheritance. This is too much for me; more especially since I have known, and known only to admire and esteem, your nephew; and if you cannot fall in with my plan as suggested in my letter, at any sacrifice to myself I am determined to replace him in his rights. I am quite aware I should do so unconditionally; but the other course would do him little harm, would meet my interests, and, what is more to your purpose, preserve yours. That is the long and the short of it. I have it off my mind now, and the decision rests entirely with you."

"A precious nice story. By heaven, sir! I'll have you arrested this very day for stealing that will."

"I have been already punished, and I doubt if I could legally be subjected to a second punishment for what was part of the offence originally punished. On the other hand, it is open to me to deny the whole transaction—to destroy the will, or, still better, to declare that it has only been discovered by me, and that I was anxious to make the communication as private as possible. You have no hold over me, Sir Roland—none whatever. I alone have the power to damage my own reputation, and, be assured, I will do so if we do not come to terms."

"You are a proper scoundrel."

"I can make every allowance for your feelings; it is hard in the decline of life, after professional failure too, to lose wealth and the social distinction which it gives, and which is, after all, not much affected by professional failure."

"You are a very particularly infernal scoundrel!" exclaimed Sir Roland, with deliberate emphasis, fully appreciating the force of Mr M'Killop's suggestive speech.

"Hard names are neither business nor argument," was the reply.

"And, by heavens! I believe the man thinks he is acting a highly virtuous part."

"There is no good arguing that point. I know I am proposing what is best for you and me, and not very harmful for your nephew. I think my conscience would be easy if you complied."

"Now, by the lord Harry! this is too much. You dare to invite me to compound a felony, and then talk about your conscience! It would not pass muster with a government chaplain of the fourth class."

“Then you decline?”

“Most certainly; and you?”

“Will communicate with your nephew at once.”

“And if money will bring you to punishment you shall be brought to it.”

“You forget that you are just resigning that very necessary instrument; but I see you are flurried, and incapable of cool reflection, so I will give you, say, twenty-four hours—that ought to be enough; if you can’t discover your own interests in that time you never will. We’ll say twenty-four hours. Perhaps I shall see you before that time elapses.”

“Never, you hypocritical hound.”

“It will be more your loss than mine in that case. Nevertheless you shall have the day of grace before I write; and now I will not detain you. If you have any more strong expressions to use, perhaps you will say them before going into the passage; it is useless to raise a scandal.”

“All the scurrilous epithets in the language are too weak to describe you,” said Sir Roland; and he banged out of the room, a very different figure from the airy gallant of an hour ago.

How that afternoon passed with the other

dramatis personæ we shall not investigate in detail. Let us stay with Sir Roland as he sat in his hotel shivering over the prospect of his annihilated fortunes, and "deeply musing upon many things." The future opened to him by M'Killop's communication was black enough in all conscience. His occupation was gone; he had no friends but such summer-day friends as would vanish with his wealth; and now that wealth was vanishing, and transferring itself to his nephew, to whom he had been always indifferent, but whom now he hated with intense cordiality, both for his high-handed defiance and for those very rights which he was bound to restore to him.

Sir Roland sat long and mused over all this. The prospect before him was as black as midnight. There was no comfort to be extracted from *it*.

There are good and evil angels, it is said, for ever around and within us, doing battle for our souls. We may suppose, therefore, that they were now engaged upon Sir Roland, each imploring him to turn his back upon the other, each praying him to go in the way each whispered was the best. It is clear that the good angel had heavy odds against him, when he could only point

to a "cold and starless road," leading painfully,
in this man's belief, to NOTHING.

Whereas the adversary could point to a broad
and sunny path leading to ease and comfort—
the horizon with all its clouds hidden by beautiful, intervening trees, whose leaves, exhaling a
Lethean fragrance, medicine all experience to
sleep, and tempt the cheated appetite again and
again to taste their glowing fruit, that for ever,
inexorably, must turn to ashes on the lips.

In this case the bad angel had a most unfair
advantage. The moral obstruction in the path
he could easily pooh-pooh, and make to appear
nothing. Sir Roland, he assured that gentleman,
had taken many far stiffer moral fences in his
time, for this was, after all, no fence at all; it
was a mere optical delusion which he could walk
through, unconscious of any extra exertion.

To drop metaphor, Sir Roland saw little moral
difficulty in the matter, and what he did see
didn't frighten him. His nephew's interests would
be inappreciably damaged—for this old ruffian
M'Killop would endow him handsomely — he
himself would give him something handsome in
the mean time, and afterwards Bertrand would
have everything. It wasn't robbing his nephew—

quite the reverse—arithmetically the thing was as square as need be.

The moral difficulty was got over simply enough. But in some dusty old corner of Sir Roland's soul there existed a fetish which he called " Honour." It has been the whim of the world for many centuries to have a sort of deity under that name : the worship is image-worship at the best ; but every worshipper graves his own particular idol which he calls by the name.

In a few points the worship may be identical with that of morality, but when to combine the worship of the two would clash with the interests of the devotee, the combination is generally abandoned for the interests.

Sir Roland's fetish was a tolerably battered rendering of the deity, and his worship principally consisted in taking the god's name in vain.

Still there it was, and somehow he felt a suspicion that to fall in with M'Killop's scheme would be to destroy this image altogether; and from a sort of antiquarian feeling or conservative prejudice, or whatever it might be, it was unpleasant to him to do so; but, after all, it was only a foolish sentiment, he felt, not to be weighed seriously against personal interest. Besides,

every man owed a duty to himself; and the word
"duty" was, as it always is, a most powerful
engine when used to back a wrong deed. It
got over that difficulty, and the fetish might be
hanged or burned.

There remained something else, however, and
here was where the shoe really pinched.

He could cook his arithmetic and his morality,
and burn his fetish easily enough; but then some
one must witness the process.

What was all right and fair when unwitnessed,
seemed to take a different shape when to be done
before another—done by the threat of another,
too—and that other a *low, base, bad man*—a
felon—a convict.

These words seemed to blaze before Sir Roland's eyes, and he said that it was impossible;
the association was too horrible. It could not
be : and so he went to bed with this sad conviction, uncheered by the smile of the good angel,
or with any happy thought of triumph over
temptation. The bad angel, however, had got
him so nearly over the obstacle, that it wasn't
likely he was going to give up his efforts at this
stage: we may conceive that Sir Roland's dreams
were carefully supervised by him.

Shall we suppose that the good influence had retired in disgust and despair?

However that may have been, it is certain that when Sir Roland rose next day and looked upon beggary by the sunlight, he would none of it; and that he betook himself, with a humbled crest, to tell his accomplice (that word had bothered him a good deal) that his terms were accepted.

M‘Killop masked, as well as he could, the satisfaction with which he saw Sir Roland enter. He knew that he could only be there for one purpose; but he affected wonder as to what could have produced the visit, considering the terms on which they had parted.

"I don't know, Mr M‘Killop," said Sir Roland, with an effort to be civil and simple, "whether I am doing right or wrong; but I have been turning over in my mind the little matters we discussed yesterday, and I really almost think that I was standing upon a punctilio when I repudiated your view so strongly."

"There is nothing like reflection, Sir Roland."

"And provided you make the reparation to my nephew which you profess yourself willing to do, I don't really see that I need distress you by an exposure."

M‘Killop laughed in his sleeve at this neat way of putting the matter, but, externally, he was grave as a judge, when he replied—

"I am very glad you take that view, Sir Roland. I felt you were speaking under the influence of excitement, and I was sure that, as a man of sense and the world, you would recall, on reflection, what you said yesterday."

"Yes," said Sir Roland, "I really think I may recall it; with a due regard to all interests and to moral obligations, I think I may venture to do so. I have to mention one or two conditions, however."

"Yes, and they are?"

"Well, I shall speak to you as a man of the world, and in that capacity you must see that it would be unpleasant to me, after your—a— unfortunate antecedents, to have any more association with you than is absolutely necessary."

"You need be under no fear of my thrusting myself upon you," was the reply.

"Very good. In the next place, I do not wish, after my nephew's intolerable insolence to me, to make the first advances to him. You or your daughter had better, then, write in the sense that I am induced to forgive him and countenance the marriage, merely out of my good-nature and innate benevolence, but that an apology is certainly due to me: you understand?"

" Certainly—nothing simpler."

" As for your daughter, she, of course, will know nothing of this little *imbroglio?*"

" Nothing, of course."

" I must say she seems a most superior young person—surprisingly so—a lady, in fact."

" You are very good to say so."

" And of course, under these circumstances, it will be possible for me to execute my duty of seeing her a good deal, and countenancing her."

" She will be very proud of your countenance, I am sure."

" Let the engagement, however, be kept strictly secret until Bertrand comes, or we hear from him."

" Certainly. I myself, since I saw you, have received a sudden call to Scotland, in connection with the property I am purchasing. Indeed I start to-day. It is most unfortunate."

Sir Roland felt that it was a very bearable calamity, and would mitigate his present lot materially.

" My daughter, however," M'Killop continued, " will manage the correspondence with Bertrand as well as I could—better, indeed. It will be a delight to her, of course, to break the news to him."

"Hum! One other question, Mr M'Killop, and I have done. Is your wife cognisant of anything we have discussed?"

"No; perfectly ignorant of the whole matter."

"And as to your little—mistake—misadventure—in early life?"

"She knows nothing of it."

"That is well; and under the circumstances it will be possible for me, when you are gone, to wait upon her as the step-mother (I think?) of my nephew's future wife."

"She will be happy to see you, I am sure."

"And now, I think, nothing further has to be said. Ah, by the by, as to the custody of the will?"

"That remains in my possession, of course," said M'Killop, with quiet decision.

"As you will; a matter of indifference. Good morning."

"Stop, Sir Roland; I am sorry to appear exacting; but, after all, business is business; and, before you go, I must ask you to sign this paper which I have drawn up."

" What is its purport ? "

" Simply the conditions of our little arrangement for the young people ; they are precisely identical with those originally proposed by me to you through your nephew—the only addition being that you, in this instrument, acknowledge that the provision is made in consideration of the temporary suspension to which Bertrand's rights are subjected."

" It appears to me to be wholly unnecessary, if you have the will."

" Perhaps so ; but, you see, one does not like an undivided *responsibility* in such a matter ; and I feel that your signature here would be a *great comfort* to me."

" And supposing I refuse ? "

" In that case, I fear, our negotiation will have been fruitless. To speak quite plainly, your signature is a *sine quâ non*."

Sir Roland reflected for a short time, with a darkened brow ; then took the paper, read it over, reflected again, and eventually said, " By this I place myself entirely in your power."

" But," replied M'Killop, " you must perceive that I shall have no object in exercising it—quite the reverse, in fact, so long as you adhere to your

part of the bargain. If you predecease me, it
shall be at once destroyed; and in case of the
other alternative, I shall have it carefully sealed
up, and an injunction inscribed on the wrapper
that it is only to be opened in case of any pecuniary disagreement with you, and to be destroyed
unopened on your decease."

Sir Roland made no farther objection, and two
servants being called in to witness his signature,
he signed the paper.

And the two worthies separated, each thinking
the other a consummate blackguard, and himself
not only shrewd, politic, and sharp, but, on the
whole, every bit as respectable as his neighbours;
which, in some neighbourhoods, might be correct
enough, of course.

That afternoon, as he had purposed, Mr
M'Killop set out for Scotland; before going,
however, he gave Eila the news of Sir Roland's
capitulation—"so that all you have to do, my
dear," he said, "is to write to Bertrand, tell
him to write a note to his uncle expressing thanks
for his kindness and regrets for his own intem-
perate language, and then set out as fast as ever
he can, to join you here; that will be fast
enough, I dare to swear. Eh? ha! ha!"

The moment Eila heard of Sir Roland's consent she began to have her very strong doubts on this point; but of course she looked as if Bertrand's ardour might be expected to lead him into remarkable feats of velocity.

"I suppose the wedding may as well come off here, Eila?" her father continued; "that would suit Sir Roland, I imagine, best of all, as he is a sort of invalid."

"I don't think it much matters, papa; and if you say and Sir Roland says it would suit to have it here, I have no objection, I am sure." Surrounded as she was with difficulties and hazards, she felt at the moment that, to get the marriage safely over, it would be a very remarkable point of detail about which *she* made a difficulty.

"Very well, I shall hurry back as quickly as I can, so as not to try your patience; and now, what am I to bring you as a wedding-gift?"

"A diamond necklace, like Lady Gramping-ton's," she said, laughing.

"You shall have it," said M'Killop, promptly.

"No, no, that won't do. It would cost thousands; besides, there are pretty certain to be family diamonds; and—— oh! I must leave it to you."

"You may depend upon getting cost, then, my dear; but I fear—I fear I can't promise much in the way of taste," said M‘Killop.

"His complaisance is wonderful," thought his daughter; "he must have been awfully set upon this marriage, and oh! what *will* happen if——" To fill up the blank even in thought was intolerable to her.

"Is Sir Roland quite pleased and kind about the matter, papa?"

"Well, he was a *leetle* bit restive at first—only at first—showed rather a pettish temper, indeed; but it soon blew over, and you will find him, no doubt, as amiable as ever. He seems to be much taken with you, Eila."

Eila was well aware of that, and entirely believed that the whole matter had been arranged by the magic of her charms.

"He will call in your absence, papa?"

"Certainly; he desires the engagement to be kept a secret till Bertrand writes or comes, however; but no doubt he will show you every civility in the mean time. Mind you write to Bertrand to-day."

Eila was not likely to forget so formidable a duty. She wrote—we have already seen the letter which she wrote, and it may well be believed that it was a work of time and anxious thought, with much mental weighing of the power of love, and much estimating of the strain which human gullibility can, under certain circumstances, be brought to bear.

CHAPTER XXXV.

It was a great relief to her when the letter to
Bertrand was fairly written and sent to the post.
She then went calmly enough down to the drawing-room to act as a sort of buffer between her
step-mamma and Sir Roland, in the event of his
calling, that lady having announced her intention
of staying in the whole afternoon on the chance,
and with the view, as she expressed it, of "putting him through his facings." Eila was too
well acquainted with the process implied by that
ill-omened phrase, to permit it to come off without supervision.

Sir Roland, however, did not come, grievously to Mrs M'Killop's disappointment, who
declared that it was "shocking bad taste," and
that she would give his Excellency "a copy of
her mind" on the earliest opportunity. She,
poor woman, had a notion that Sir Roland's un-

expected complaisance was mainly due to the discovery of their high social position, and the reputation which she believed herself to have acquired as a leader of the fashion in Pau, and she would "just let him see what she considered due to herself as the girl's step-mother."

Sir Roland simply stayed away because he had not quite made up his mind as to the line he should take with his two future connections. In the course of the next twenty-four hours he had done so, however, and accordingly presented himself, the next afternoon, to pay his respects.

Three months ago, or in the Cairnarvoch district, where Sir Roland would have been, so to speak, in his own particular sphere of domination, Mrs M'Killop would have looked forward to meeting him in a very different spirit. But in her case the old proverb, "cœlum, non animum, mutant," &c., was discredited. At home, she was nobody but the wife of a rich unknown lessee of a country residence in a district where her wealth was rather an outrage to local sensibilities, provoking the hostility and sarcasms of a genteel, and therefore rather an envious, poverty. It would be different, she assured herself, when the lordship of Tolmie-Donnochie was a *fait ac-*

compli—and to a certain extent she was right; for " the dirty acres " have a very superior effect, particularly on the landed mind, to that produced by the coined currency; for many reasons, and among others, perhaps, that an investment in the one appears to imply a superabundance of the other, and is, at the same time, by no means of such a volatile essence.

Up to this time, however, there had been no dirty acres, and Mrs M'Killop had been quite aware that her position was not good. But here in Pau she had burst, as it were, into a new sphere—she was received, and made much of, even by a large society, who accepted as sufficient, the tangible evidences of her wealth which they saw, without troubling themselves about acres or anything else, which could do them no good; while she, incapable of nice social discrimination, accepted flash manners and florid assumption as evidences of the highest *ton*, and implicitly believed in the Irish castles and the *châteaux en Espagne*, which gave territorial distinction to so many of her circle. His very quality of pretender makes a pretender who has been long about the world, all the quicker in detecting others who are in the same line; but a pretender who has only exercised his function on a parochial scale, swallows the brag of co-professionals with a voraciousness unknown to otherwise simpler folks.

So Mrs M'Killop, believing herself to be quite the apex of a fashionable set, was much uplifted.

"And if," she said to herself, "Sir Roland, who has boggled about the marriage, imagines that he is doing us any honour, or is going to attempt to patronise *me*, I will take care to put him in his right place." With erected crest, therefore, and all her peacock plumage on the perpendicular, she expected the interview.

Sir Roland had thought his part over with much care and deliberation, and since the marriage was a necessity, he had quite determined to make the very best of it to the world, when it was divulged. The tone he determined to take was, that his nephew had been foolish, perhaps, but that the girl was really in herself of such beauty, fascination, and refinement, and, above all, had such immense prospects, that he had felt constrained to sanction the affair, though, of course, she would be kept away from her own people, who were not quite,—you understand, &c.; and therefore, after all, the advantages of the marriage would greatly counterbalance the disadvantages. Things of the sort were done now every day, dukes setting the example; the *sangre azul* would stand a little adulteration, particularly when it was handsomely paid to do so. Such was the tone he would adopt to society.

As to Eila, he had resolved to be affable and charming to her, and to let his airy gallantry slide imperceptibly into the playful affection of an elderly relative.

Of her step-mother's idiosyncrasies he knew nothing, and if he had, it would only have confirmed him in his decision, that, as it was part of his compact to have no relations with her husband, he need, and would, have nothing to do with her either; he would civilly ignore her, in fact, and keep her in her right place.

Mrs M'Killop, it will thus be seen, had resolved upon aggressive action with him, while his towards her was to be defensive. He was to be put in his, she was to be kept in her, place. Eila, meanwhile, had resolved to act as circumstances inspired her.

The ladies were both in the drawing-room when Sir Roland entered, which he did with outstretched hands and a rapid step, as if consumed with impatience to assure his future niece of his congratulations. In a moment both her hands were in his, and he was provisionally availing himself, with much apparent gusto, of an uncle's privilege of salute.

"And I never guessed! never dreamed!" he exclaimed, holding her back from him with an admiring gaze for a moment, and then repeating the salute—"never guessed, as how should I, by the by? Ah! fair Aurora, you conquered at once; the stupid, prudent, cantankerous old martinet of an uncle dropped his weapons in a moment. I thought my nephew a fool; I now know that he is a doosed sensible fellow, and the luckiest dog in Christendom—luckiest dog in Christendom, I declare. *Entre nous*, I only heard it in time for my own safety; another twenty - four hours and my fate was sealed. That's a secret though, ha! ha! We must not tell Bertrand that; make him jealous, eh? ha! ha! If you had refused the old uncle,—figure it to yourself—the situation, eh? hum!"

"Supposing the old uncle had *not* been refused, though?"

"What? jilt the nephew for the uncle, eh?

he! he! Ah! you little flatterer, if I thought *that*—upon my conscience if I thought *that*—I would go by to-night's mail to England and assassinate the dog—I would, without a scruple—I swear it."

" I am afraid you are a dreadful flatterer, Sir Roland."

" With you, my dear child, flattery is impossible."

All this time Mrs M'Killop (whom Sir Roland had only noticed by a deep reverence, on entering) had been bridling and boiling up on her sofa, waiting for recognition; but, at this point, as Sir Roland seated himself confidentially beside Eila, she deemed that the moment had come for action.

" Eila !" she exclaimed, in a loud, husky voice; and, as the young lady was too much absorbed to notice or reply, she repeated still louder, " Eila, I say ! "

Sir Roland put up his glass and half whispered, " The lady wants to speak to you, my dear."

Eila looked up, " Well, Mrs M'Killop," she said.

" Well, Miss M'Killop," repeated the step-dame, " does it not occur to you to introjooce this—this *gentleman* to *me* who is doing *you* the favour to visit you in *my* drawing-room?"

"Oh! I beg your pardon—Sir Roland Cameron, Mrs M'Killop."

Mrs M'Killop rose and executed a series of Elizabethan antics intended to represent a dignified curtsey. Sir Roland also rose and made a solemn obeisance.

"You are just arrived in Paw, Sir Rawland, I believe?" she began, loftily.

"I have been about forty-eight hours in Pau, I think," said Sir Roland, studying Mrs M'Killop and all her strange tints of complexion and apparel curiously through his eye-glass.

"You were fortunate to catch M'Killop here before his departure for Scotland."

"I—eh? who? I beg your pardon."

"Papa, you know," explained Eila.

"Ah! yes, of course; he has gone away, has he?"

"He has gone to *Tolmie-Donnochie.*" The word came forth with the guttural thunder of an avalanche.

"Indeed, in—in—in Russia, is it?"

"No, sir, it is our property in the north; not a great distance from your own, Sir Rawland."

" Oh, indeed! wasn't aware; my habits have been those of an absentee," said Sir Roland, recognising a fresh reason for keeping them so.

" It is a new purchase, but it is part of an old family property of *my* ancestors," continued the lady.

" Ah, indeed!"

" The M'Whannels."

" Oh!"

" Of Glenspishach."

" Hum!"

Neither Tolmie-Donnochie nor its ancient proprietors seemed to produce any adequate effect upon Sir Roland; so she opened a new vein.

" You will scarcely have made many acquaintances as yet in Paw, I preshoom?"

" I have made none except that of my charming young friend here," and he beamed, as it were antithetically, upon Eila.

" There is a good society here—very good—this, they say, is a particularly good year. The Morrissy-Moloneys having come back makes a difference. They found Nice vulgar and stupid last year. You may have met them?"

"I have not had that advantage."

"They are people of *tong* and distinction. We are inseparables."

"Indeed!"

"I look forward to paying a long visit next summer at their lovely castle Morrissy, and they will be with us at Tolmie - Donnochie in the shooting season."

"Ah!"

"We shall be quite a Paw party there. The Fortnum-Redmaynes, Count Horneyhoff, and also Baron Hunkers, have agreed to come, instead of shooting in their own forests; isn't it good of them?"

"The Count's forest is not very far from Homburg, I fancy."

"Ah! you know about him?"

"I suspect I have met a good many of his family about the world."

"Indeed! He is most attractive; and dear Hunkers quite the original—so simple and absent: fancy his carrying away good Mr Moloney's snuff-box from the card-table, without the least knowing it, t'other evening. The laugh was entirely against Moloney, however, for the box turned out to be *brass*—it is a freak of his to carry a brass box. And the Baron brought it back, and said so *knavely*, ' The next time I will take a smell of it, before I steal.' "

" It was scarcely a remunerative evening for the Baron," said Sir Roland.

" If I can be of any use in getting you into the best circle, I shall be glad. The Morrissy-Moloneys give their ball to-night. I think I may say that my introduction will be quite sufficient, if you like to take charge of me and Eila."

" The temptation to take charge of you, my dear child," said Sir Roland, turning to Eila, " is all but irresistible, yet I must decline; I am engaged."

" Oh ! put it off," cried Mrs M'Killop. " Everything in Paw gives way to the Morrissy-Moloneys."

" I'm afraid my party would scarcely understand such an excuse. I fear they are not quite in the Morrissy-Moloney circle."

" All the easier to say ' No.' "

" It would spoil my friends' rubber, and I should lose my own."

" Oh ! as far as whist goes, you'll get that at the Morrissy-Moloneys ; Baron Hunkers is crazy about whist ; and your friends won't mind when they know what set you are going to."

"All my little appointments at present are made of gold, and the Baron might have a fit of absence. No, no; I think I can scarcely throw over the Duchess and Lady Grampington for your distinguished friends. Thanks, all the same."

The Duchess and Lady Grampington! Theirs was a sphere to which Mrs M'Killop never dreamt of raising her eyes.

The Pau lofty social elevation from which she meant to patronise Sir Roland—as the only platform open to her for such a feat—suddenly shrunk down to the dimensions of a mole-hill, and she was staring up at him, open-mouthed, from that slight and rather dirty eminence. He had only been there forty-eight hours, and he was whisting with the "Dii majorum gentium" already!

"Oh!" was all she could say, her face becoming of a deep peony colour. She had put Sir Roland through his facings, and in his right place. His manner had been cool and half amused, but perfectly civil throughout. He had expected that the woman, from her first onslaught, would require some rough handling, and her sudden and total collapse rather surprised him—a collapse rendered the more palpable from her making an excuse to leave the room at this juncture. Sir Roland seized the opportunity of her absence to explain to Eila certain points as to their future relative positions.

"I am sorry," he said, "I can't ask the ladies I have mentioned to be attentive to you as yet. When the engagement, which your father wished to be kept quiet till Bertrand arrived" (Sir Roland's memory seemed singularly treacherous to-day) "is given out, I shall do so; but of course any attention they may pay you will be meant for you alone as *my* future relative, and is not to be supposed to include any of—of—your *former* connections. And, my dear child, *entre nous*, the foreign noblemen, and the Irish magnates are no doubt very charming, and their eccentricities delightful, though at times expensive; but it is *de rigueur* that your acquaintance with them should be dropped as early as possible, *if* my friends are to have the happiness of your society. The whims and caprices of people are unaccountable in social matters, and I fear the Duchess and Lady Grampington, and indeed all my friends, are full of caprices of the sort. I almost think, for instance, that the frolics of

Baron Hunkers would not amuse them—you understand me?"

"Perfectly; but these are Mrs M‘Killop's friends, not mine. I shall have no difficulty in dropping them at once, therefore," said Eila.

"Excellent! and now, my dear, let us talk over our little family matters. You have written to Bertrand?"

"Yes."

"You know the young rascal really sent me a most impertinent letter?"

"Yes, indeed; I am so sorry, and I was the cause."

"Say no more—that is his excuse; I forgave him the instant I knew the cause."

"You are too kind and delightful by far."

"Bertrand would have been jilted for me, that is evident. I protest I shall hate him for ever." One of the truths spoken in jest, it is to be suspected.

"You know that I *quite* refused to have anything to do with him, after your letter, until we should hear if you would relent?"

"The little fabricator!" thought Sir Roland; adding aloud, "You will make a model wife."

“And niece, I hope,” with *such* a winning smile that his Excellency again took the privileges of an uncle, in advance.

And so the dialogue went on most swimmingly between the future relatives ; Sir Roland succeeding in establishing exactly the footing he aimed at. As for poor Mrs M‘Killop, she, on her return to the room, sat, feeling very sore and sulky, and *quite* in her place. The visit was brought to a close by the announcement of Count Corrigan-Shaughnessy (Shannochbawn)— a blinky and not very clean-looking young man, with a foamy head of hair, and a roll of music in his hand, who entered the room in the heraldic attitude of *passant regardant*, his body making for Mrs M‘Killop, while his eyes and head devoted themselves to Eila.

“ He is in the Pope’s Noble Guard,” whispered Eila.

“ He combines every Continental advantage, then,” replied his Excellency—“ an Irishman (I presume), a count, and a captain. Thanks, no —no presentation.” He buttoned up his pockets with a comical look, and made his adieux with affectionate *empressement* to Eila, but including

the Count and Mrs M'Killop in a formal reverence. "Till to-morrow, Eila; I will call for
you after lunch, if you like, and take you for a
drive—would you care?"

"I should delight in it."

"Very well, till then, adieu."

CHAPTER XXXVI.

THE next few days passed off somewhat in the following fashion. Sir Roland was most attentive to Eila—driving her out, accompanying her in her rides, walking with her in the Park, or attending her in the Place, when the band played. He never ventured within the M'Killop walls, however, and his attendance on Eila was tacitly understood to be conditional on the absence of her step-dame.

They did not meet in the evenings. Eila, indeed, did not quite see the advantage of drawing off from the society in which she was a particular star, until a substitute was open to her, and only stayed away from those parties which were undeniably of the baser sort; but Sir Roland spent this part of his day in the small and select coterie to which he had the *entrée*, and to which she had not. The Pau gossips

were, of course, at their wits' ends to account for
all the strange phenomena connected with Sir
Roland's intercourse with Eila ; but their various
solutions we need not waste time in chronicling.
She kept her own counsel, it need hardly be
said, and Mrs M'Killop was under her husband's
strict injunctions to do the same—a circumstance
which had latterly come to have some weight
with her ; besides, to have bruited the marriage,
when she was so evidently ignored by the bridegroom's principal relative, would have been unpleasant. " When Bertrand comes," she said to
herself, " I shall not be treated so vilely." And
so she held her tongue—*en attendant*.

The slight badinage which Sir Roland met
with from his distinguished friends, on his public
appearances with the young beauty, he had little
difficulty in parrying. It was pleasant to him,
in fact. It had always been his *rôle* to be
a " sad dog" among the sex ; and to take up
that of the evergreen, on his return to Europe,
was by no means disagreeable to him.

And so the days passed on ; Eila finding her
future uncle the most charming of men—so kind,
so considerate, so lavish of promises for the future,
so lively and entertaining, that she never felt dull

with him for a moment. Although, when away from him—when alone—when she allowed a certain grim contingency, with all its direful consequences, to throw its shadow across her thoughts—she was not dull certainly, for her feelings were simply those of desperation. If any one could have looked into her mind at such moments, and seen all its tumults and anxieties, he would have regarded her radiant aspect in public with amazement, and something even of admiration. She was living, as it were, within a bubble, owing much of her ornamental aspect to its prismatic colours, and conscious that a breath might, even then, be travelling towards her, which would dissolve that frail surrounding. It was a critical position for a young lady to be in, and yet carry so brave a front withal.

Let us go back to Bournemouth, and see whether a breath to dissolve the bubble was really to travel from its shore.

When we left Bertrand and his friend, they had just adjourned, until the morrow, the consideration of Eila's letter and the form which Bertrand's answer to it should take. When the morrow came, however, and the matter was opened, Pigott found that his friend's mind was already quite made up, and that he had resolved simply to write to Eila, and tell her that he had considered her former letter as finally breaking off their engagement, and that no circumstance had intervened to make him take a different view of the subject. He had determined, also, to leave her to make what explanation she pleased to her father, being satisfied that, in her own interest, she would not compromise him by the manner of doing so. Further, as his uncle had not thought proper to renew relations with him directly, he would not take the initiative in bringing about a reconciliation.

Such were his fixed resolves, and it was in vain that his friend combated them, pointing out that, in justice to himself, he was bound to let Mr M'Killop understand why he declined to go on with the marriage, and that the chances were, he would only aggravate the eventual exposure which Eila's conduct was certain to undergo, by being obliged to meet an action for breach of promise. As to his neglecting the opportunity of a reconciliation with his uncle, that, in Pigott's view, was almost indicative that the fever had permanently weakened his friend's brain. But all his arguments and expostulations were useless;

and Bertrand cut them short by sitting down to write the letter, according to his own plan.

It was short and very much to the purpose, and ran as follows :—

" Your letter of the —th has reached me, and I will not trouble you with a long answer to it. The very great misconception of my character which could alone have induced you to write this second letter, is perfectly consistent with a statement in your former one, that you had no great belief in your own love for me. It certainly would justify a feeling of contempt, rather than of love ; but you are apparently indifferent to this, and willing, notwithstanding, to ally yourself with the very simple person you take me to be. Your former letter, however, perfectly satisfied me that we are quite unsuited to one another; and this would only confirm that impression, if confirmation were at all necessary. And when I assure you that I am not quite a simpleton, and that I value and respect truth beyond all qualities, I think you will understand, without any broad speaking, why further relations between us are impossible. I have determined not to write to your father. If I did write, I should, in justice to myself, be compelled to speak in plainer terms. You may account to him for my decision, in any way you please, consistent with the fact that I have not wantonly violated my engagement.

"I have only farther to add that I have undergone not a little pain and sorrow at your hands. I am neither too proud to own this, nor so poor in spirit as to reproach you with it, but I shall be glad if the confession has any effect in influencing your future conduct to others, and if you also extract, as I do, some wholesome lesson from what has passed between us.

"BERTRAND CAMERON."

The spirit, though not the letter of this, Bertrand communicated to his friend, who pronounced it to be a masterpiece of Quixotic folly.

"She deserves a deal more plain speaking," he said; "and the whole clan M'Killop ought to know what a little serpent is nestling in the folds of their tartan. However, it is a mere matter of time, and you will have to do as I advise in the long-run, with the difference that you will have to pay for the process a good many six-and-eight-pences into the bargain. May they be very many.

It will serve you right. As to your uncle, why, that branch of the imbecility simply sickens me ; that's all. If ever there was a case of cutting off a nose to spite a face, here it is. Oh dear ! oh dear ! I am the object of very few mercies, but for this one I desire to be thankful—that I was not born a Celt."

" I could only reply with a *tu quoque*, my dear fellow, which I scorn ; so let us say no more about it. I have signed and sealed this my act and deed. I am now going to deliver it to the post-office ; and, at the same time, I will pay my respects to Miss Grant, if you will give me her address."

" I will go with you, and show the way."

" No, no ; I shall have to tell her about this affair more or less minutely, and a third party would be *de trop*."

" I'll go with you to the door, at all events. Between ourselves, Bertrand, I would tell her as nearly the truth of the matter as your Quixotic soul can bring itself to do. It can never displease any well-regulated young lady to hear that her step-sister is a *mauvais sujet*. Besides, this girl is of the right sort ; and she may be of use hereafter in flavouring the other young lady's romantic account of the matter with some spice of the truth. She may even save you the breach of promise case—who knows? Be open with her, most noble M'Quixote."

"Come along in the mean time, most sapient of Sassenachs."

As luck would have it, long before they reached the house where Morna was visiting, they espied her in the distance, walking slowly by herself in a solitary path among the pine-groves, "*A la bonne heure!*" said Bertrand, "Leave me, Pigott, and I will give chase. Nothing could be more fortunate." Whereupon the two friends separated.

Before that eventful day when Bertrand Cameron waited upon Mr M'Killop in his business-room at Cairnarvoch to ask him formally to sanction his engagement with Eila, we have Mr M'Killop's own statement on record, that no idea of such a solution of the problem how to reconcile the whispers of conscience with the dictates of his own interest, had crossed his mind.

Any statement from such a source is, of course, liable to grave suspicion; but it is more than probable that, in this case, he spoke the truth. We must remember that he led a solitary life,

and mingled but little with the rest of the circle.
We must also remember that he was a man not
likely to be much versed in the ways of woman-
kind ; and therefore, that what he did see of
what went on at Cairnarvoch, when Eila was
playing her elaborate game and employing Mr
Tainsh and his misplaced passion as a fulcrum,
was not very likely to enlighten him as to the
real state of matters.

The fact of the matter was, that the sight of
Bertrand Cameron for the first time, made the
wrong he was doing much more tangible to him ;
and that, instead of plotting a compromise, his
better nature was struggling with his worse to
decide, once for all, to do what was right, and
make the declaration.   But duty has an uphill
task to perform, when, in opposing self-interest,
it is only backed by a moral principle, weak at
best, and become somewhat decrepit from want
of air and exercise.   The devil's own middle
course of procrastination, paved with the best
intentions, is the course, at best, generally pursued under such circumstances, and M'Killop
adopted it, deceiving and, even while he deceived,
tormenting, himself.   As a relief under the circumstances—to assure himself, as it were, that

his act of justice was but temporarily postponed
—he was in the habit of writing letters to Bertrand informing him of his rights, and stating
that the proof of them lay in his hands. These
letters he of course destroyed, one by one; but
the writing of them served as a sort of anodyne
for the inflammation of his conscience; and, as
one of them was always in existence, he laid
great stress on the fact that, if anything happened to him, Bertrand would not be defrauded
of his rights.

But the moment Bertrand came forward as a
suitor for his daughter's hand, he saw how a
compromise might be effected; and his attenu-
ated moral principle could offer no resistance.
He resolved, therefore, to discontinue his one-
sided correspondence, which would otherwise
have probably gone on till the day of his death;
and it was the last of that celebrated collection
which fell into the hands of Morna Grant, under
the circumstances already detailed, on the night
of Bertrand's proposal. The possession of this
secret had sorely disquieted Morna all along, for
there was no attenuation about *her* moral principle; and, when she heard that the marriage had
become a matter of uncertainty, her anxiety and

disquietude largely increased. She had seen at a glance, that the restitution of Bertrand in his rights was, somehow or other, grievously counter to Mr M'Killop's interests and inclinations; and she had felt that pressure would be necessary on her part, to bring it about.

On hearing, therefore, that the marriage was jeopardised, she wrote to Mr M'Killop in a very decided tone, insisting upon being informed what further limit he claimed for his concealment. Her letter troubled him not a little, for he saw that even when the marriage was a *fait accompli*, some especially well-devised fable of a compromise between uncle and nephew would be necessary to satisfy so conscientious an observer. His answer was of course "Time;" that the marriage would come off certainly; and that, until it did, secrecy was indispensable.

As to Morna, she had felt compelled to be satisfied with his assurance, and waited on, with an uneasy mind. But yesterday had brought her a letter from Mr M'Killop, informing her that Sir Roland's consent had finally removed all obstacles to the marriage, so the period of her complicity in a guilty secret was apparently nearly terminated, and she had felt a corresponding relief.

Under all the circumstances, it is not surprising that on this morning, as she strolled about the sylvan pathways, her maiden meditations should be a good deal devoted to him who was even now in quest of her. The marriage was now coming off, and she need no longer feel like a receiver of his stolen goods; she might now think of him without a pang of shame. The marriage was coming off, and all the connection that, unknown to him, had existed between them, would now terminate. Was there nothing else that the marriage would finally extinguish? Had he never been strongly in her thoughts in any other connection than with this odious secret? If he had not, how was it that her thoughts wandered back, and dwelt, with something more than a sweet pain, on the early days of their acquaintance? on those pleasant hours by the river—on those twilight hours on the terrace — on that quick sympathy and understanding that had risen up between them, amid music and laughter, and the free interchange of their vagrant thoughts?

There can be no doubt that poor Morna had

had her little excursion into fairy-land — conducted thither by a beautiful prince—and that the counter-magic of a hostile enchantress had sent her back to the cold world, and robbed her of the dear companionship. How brief had been the bright illusion! how complete and sudden its departure! for it was all gone, leaving nothing behind but an aching void in her heart, and a blush of maidenly shame on her honest, innocent face; no indignation against any one; neither spite, nor envy, nor any such thing. She was humbled, but it was by her own act: merely, she assured herself, as the result of her own folly and presumption. "Who was I to attract *him?*" was her thought. "No rival was necessary; he never did think, and never could have thought, of me, but as an uncouth girl, who might amuse him as a *pis-aller*, when there was nothing else to be done. When she came, I saw it at once. Even his first manner to her was so utterly different; and I was instantly forgotten. He might have spoken to me a little; but I was too insignificant; and it was evidently by an effort of good-nature and good-breeding, that he contrived to show me that he remembered my existence at all. Yes, I have been very foolish and very wrong, and I could die of shame if I thought he suspected; but he does not. Oh no, he cannot. How he would despise me if he knew that I had this secret about his fortune. It would look like spite. It is intolerable. I could contain it no longer if the marriage was not to come off immediately. But it is coming off, and there is an end of my—my misery. I shall be at peace again."

In the midst of these thoughts, she heard her name pronounced by a voice, the sound of which arrested her as if her heart had stopped beating, and turning, she was confronted by Bertrand. Her agitation was great, and naturally so, under the circumstances. It was quite unconcealable, and Bertrand noticed it, saying, as he held out his hand, "I beg a thousand pardons, Miss Grant, for coming on you like a footpad. I fear I have startled you."

"I was a little startled," she murmured; "it was very foolish of me. I never heard you coming; and I have not been very strong lately."

"I am really very sorry, but I remembered you had the nerves of a mountaineer, or I would have been more careful." His own illness had

revealed to him for the first time the existence
of nerves.

"Pray don't apologise," said Morna; "it was
nothing.   I hope you are quite recovered."

"Thank you; I am quite an impostor now, to
be playing the invalid, and I am going back to
my duty soon."

Morna observed a great change in his appearance.   He had no longer the air of an invalid,
but what he had gone through had given him a
much older look.   His features were sharper,
and the lines of his face more strongly defined,
and his expression had lost its quick vivacity.

"I am afraid you have had a very serious
illness," she said.

"Yes, it was serious enough while it lasted, I
believe; but one shakes these things off quickly
enough."

"You are not old enough to be offended by
being told that you look a great deal older than
when I last saw you.   You *do* look years older.
You must have been very ill."

"I feel years older, Miss Grant," he said
quickly, and then went on, "I was on my way
to call upon you just now, when I saw you in the
distance."

"You are very kind; we can turn down this path—that will take us home."

"If you have no objection to let me escort you for a little in your walk, I would rather do so than go to your friend's house just now. I have, in fact, something to speak to you about privately, and we shall be more private here. Have you any objection?"

"None," said Morna, faintly, and they walked along together in silence—her thought being that he had got a clue to the secret, and was come to cross-examine her.

They walked on for a little in silence; and at last Bertrand spoke with an effort. "I daresay, Miss Grant, you divine what I wish to speak about?"

Morna could make no reply. She was about to be arraigned, tried, and convicted as a receiver of stolen goods.

"At any rate," he went on, "I need not trouble you with a preface. I have come to speak to you about my—my marriage, Miss Grant."

"Oh!" said Morna, with something like a sob of relief; "and—and—I am glad to hear that I have now to congratulate you."

“ Captain Pigott told me you were under this impression, and I have lost no time in hastening to undeceive you.”

“ Undeceive me !” ejaculated Morna, stopping in the sudden tumult of her thoughts. “ What? how? Is it again postponed?”

“ As far as I am concerned it was finally and utterly broken off, months ago.”

“ And will not now take place ? ” she inquired.

“ Never, certainly.”

She looked at him in dumb amazement ; all the consequences of this state of things—all the entanglements of her situation—the secret again —the difficult duties she would have to perform, even the wild hopes that but now had seemed so dead and gone for ever—all rushed over her mind together in one tumultuous flood, and over-whelmed her. She could say nothing but repeat mechanically his words, “ Never, certainly.”

“ I see you are astonished,” he continued, “ and naturally suppose that I am grievously to blame—that this is my doing. Miss Grant, it is none of my doing, or I would not be here beside you now.”

“ I do not understand,” faltered Morna. “ I had a letter.”

"I know you had, but a letter which deceived you."

"Good heavens! is it possible that he could have deceived me for the purpose of——"

"I do not say that Mr M'Killop deceived you; indeed I am certain that he was himself deceived. I will tell you, in as few words as possible, how matters stand. When I said that the termination of the engagement was by no act of mine, I did not speak quite correctly; I should have said rather, that it was terminated by no blamable act of mine."

"But—but it is not understood by Eila to be terminated at all. Mr M'Killop writes that she is so happy in the prospect of the marriage—the immediate prospect."

"I will explain that presently. Miss M'Killop discovered, some months ago, that she had mistaken her feelings, and that her affection for me was not proof against the obvious inconvenience of marrying a disinherited husband; for you must know that I had accepted the disinheritance with which I was threatened if I persevered in my engagement with her. You must understand that I had done so, however, without consulting her, for reasons which I need not mention now,

and I found that I had made a mistake. It
would almost seem that it was my inheritance,
and not myself, that she had intended to marry;
for, when the one went, her feelings changed,
and she told me that our engagement must
terminate. It did terminate, then, as far as I
was concerned, finally. By some unaccountable
change, the prohibition, which had forbidden the
marriage under pains and penalties, seems to have
been removed—my disinheritance would appear
to be cancelled—and, logically enough, from her
point of view, Miss M'Killop seems to assume
that, by that circumstance, our engagement is
renewed. As I am not a mere puppet, however,
I take a different view, and I have written to tell
her so. There were also circumstances connected
with the rupture of our engagement, which entirely altered my view of her character, and
made it impossible for me not to consider that I
had made an escape, rather than sustained a loss.
I will not, however, pain you and myself by going
into details. But, in justice to Mr M'Killop, it
is necessary that I should tell you that his
daughter has evidently all along deceived him
with the idea that the engagement was only in
abeyance; and I may say that it was necessary

for her to do so, to prevent the discovery that her conduct to me had been what she might probably be ashamed to own. There, Miss Grant, is briefly the real state of the case."

"It is astounding and incomprehensible to me," said Morna, rather thinking aloud than addressing Bertrand.

"I will, however, pledge my word of honour as a gentleman, that I have given you a true, and as mild as possible a version of the story."

"I never doubted that for an instant, Mr Cameron—but have you written to Mr M'Killop?"

"I have not. I could not write to him without giving him, as the young lady's father, a complete and detailed account of his daughter's line of conduct. In my own justification, I could not do so; but I am anxious to spare him, and even her, unnecessary pain; so I have left it to Miss M'Killop to explain the rupture, in any way she pleases that shall leave me clear from the charge of having violated my engagement, and as blameless in appearance, as I am in fact."

"But you *must* write to Mr M'Killop," cried Morna, vehemently.

"I cannot see why."

"There must be no more delay, doubt, or deception—he *must* have it from you direct."

"Why?"

"For his sake, for your sake, for the sake of honour and honesty."

"I think my honour will be sufficiently guarded. Miss M'Killop will scarcely venture to misrepresent me. If she does, please remember what I have said, and call upon me for the proof."

"Oh, it is not that! Oh, if it was only that! What *am* I to do? Who will tell me what is right?"

Bertrand looked at her in surprise. Her manner was much excited—unaccountably so.

"I do not understand your allusion, Miss Grant; but pray do not distress yourself any further. All has been said that need be said. Let us change this unhappy subject. No amount of words can alter it."

"Oh, yes, yes, much has to be said, and everything has to be altered, and I have to do it—but how? how? I wish to do my duty. God knows I do. But what is it?"

Her mind seemed to be wandering strangely, and Bertrand, in great perplexity, again begged her, with soothing words, to dismiss the subject from her mind and allow him to escort her home.

"No, no," she cried, "not till I have spoken. I am absolved from my engagement now, for the marriage is never to come off. I *must* speak, and I *will*. Listen, Mr Cameron, I have a secret about you."

"About me, Miss Grant? That seems strange. Not a very important one, I fancy."

"Yes, an important one—of the greatest importance to you—affecting your fortune and your career, and which I have had in my keeping, Heaven knows how unwillingly, all these months. You will hate and despise me, perhaps, for having kept it; but I was bound—bound by a promise—to keep it, until the arrangements for your marriage were completed,—until you were married to my step-sister. I believe I ought to have made no such promise; but there were many circumstances; and oh! it is so hard, so difficult, to know how to act, when one is groping in the dark, not knowing whether what appears the right direction may not turn out the wrong one, and whether to take it may not be to mislead and compromise the interests of others. But the time has come—the limit of my compact has been reached—and right or wrong, I *will* speak. I can endure the burden no longer."

"I am sure you are agitating yourself most unnecessarily, Miss Grant. There is little that can damage the fortunes of a man further, when he is ruined."

"Not ruined, Mr Cameron,—there is the secret. You are being unjustly kept out of your fortune, yours by birthright; and I have been conniving at it for months past. What do you think of me?"

Morna's excitement was great; and Bertrand thought to himself, that this poor girl was certainly under some delusion—partially deranged. The commonest form of insanity is this upon the subject of " rights," so he said to her—

"My dear Miss Grant, another time you will tell me of this; but kindly delay the communication. I am still a little weak, and would rather defer unnecessary agitation. Suppose we return now?"

"No, no, no; it is not unnecessary agitation; and I will not defer it. Listen to me!" and she told Bertrand her story, with which we are already acquainted.

He soon saw, as she proceeded, that it was

no creation of a disordered fancy she was reporting, and he heard her to the end without interruption.

It was a communication that might have moved any one profoundly, and a sordid soul would have been transported with exultation at the sudden access of fortune, at such a time and in such a mode, carrying with it the downfall of one who had cast him off with scorn and contumely.

But Bertrand's first eager question was, "Did it appear that my uncle was aware of all this?"

"No," said Morna, "he is quite ignorant of it."

"Thank Heaven! the honour of our name is untarnished. How could I doubt it?"

"Can you forgive me for my part in it?" said Morna.

"Forgive you, Miss Grant! There is nothing to forgive. It appears to me that one who opens the door of fortune to you, and says 'Walk in,' does not require to make many apologies. It is gratitude I owe you, nothing else; and I am grieved indeed that you have suffered so much distress, more especially since that very distress springs from a tender sense of honour which, believe me, I appreciate. You were bound to keep your promise till the condition was fulfilled or became impossible, and I am only not sure that you have done right in anticipating Mr M'Killop."

"Oh, do not blame—do not blame me! If you knew, if you only knew, how I have weighed and balanced and argued it, over and over, from one side to another, till my head was nearly turned, you would not blame me."

"My dear Miss Grant, nothing is farther from my thought than to blame you, and here is an expedient which will set everything to rights. I will delay taking any action in the matter till Mr M'Killop has time to make the communication to me himself, and he shall never know from me that he is not my first informant. Will that satisfy you?"

"Oh, thank you—thank you! how good you are! There can be no harm in that, can there?"

"None whatever, undoubtedly."

"Then my mind is at rest—what a burden it has been! I can hardly believe that it is removed. If Mr M'Killop does not do what is right, then my communication will not have been premature."

"But have you any doubts of him? Forgive the question."

"To speak the plain truth, it was evident that

it would be a most stupendous effort to him to make the declaration, and the very thought of it seemed to agitate him deeply; why, I cannot understand, more particularly when your interests were to be bound up with his, to a certain extent."

"It is certainly most mysterious; and how he comes to have this intelligence exclusively, still more so; but I am sure he will do his duty."

"I fervently hope so. And now I think I must go in. Good-bye."

"Good-bye; but I hope you will allow me to come and see you. You are not going to leave Bournemouth yet, are you?"

"No, not yet. In a week or ten days I am to accompany Mr M'Killop to Pau; but I do not think it could be a pleasure to you to come and see me, considering all the associations I must be connected with in your mind. I think this had better be our last meeting."

Poor Morna felt that it had better be so, for many reasons; the words came from the bitter wisdom of her heart, yet his answer, in spite of herself, was pleasant to her.

"I have no association in my mind with you but what is of the pleasantest description, Miss

Grant : if we rejected everything good in this
world because of its possible suggestions from
mere proximity, it appears to me that the good
that is in the world would be altogether un-
enjoyed."

"Oh, but I am not good ; and, so far from it,
that, as to this secret, I did not even know what
part a good person would have acted."

"Your mind may be very easy on that point.
I owe you a debt of gratitude.   It seems possible
that, but for you, I might never have heard of
my rights at all."

"You can't owe me gratitude for doing what
was right—for doing it so feebly, too ; gratitude
for speaking the truth ! when to withhold it
would have been misery to myself !   Oh no,
you owe me no gratitude, Mr Cameron."

"You take a humbler view of yourself than I
do, Miss Grant.   Truth lies in a well, you know,
it is said.   But it is not every one who will take
the trouble and risk of descending, to bring it up.
I may call, may I not ?   I assure you that my
old friendship is only very much strengthened by
what has occurred, and I shall be proud of your
friendship, if you will let me have it."

"If you care to call, I shall always be glad to see you. Thank you for all the kind things you have said to me. Good-bye."

She held out her hand, and there came back to her face the look of happy, kindly frankness that had made it so winning, before the shadows of the past months had fallen upon her.

CHAPTER XXXVII.

BERTRAND carried his strange news to Pigott, who at once took the view that M'Killop had been playing a deep game all along, and withholding the intelligence till Bertrand was fairly "landed;" no doubt thinking that the possession of a fortune makes a man fastidious in his matrimonial views. "It was a plant all along from the beginning, you may depend upon it, Bertrand," he said; "he had got the intelligence, and, being a freebooter, he was not going to part with it gratis: he scented you out when you lay on your form at Gosport, and the way in which he got you into the toils was most creditable. Upon my life, I respect old M'Killop!

"The shooting was a plant. The very manner in which the young lady was brought into action —not too hurriedly, you remember—was a *tour de force* in itself. Tainsh was a 'bonnet,' and all this mysterious juggle of negotiating with the uncle, was the height of art.

"He must be a thundering clever fellow; and such a masterpiece that wooden, stolid expression of his! The cunning old mole! His daughter must have lost her cue somehow, and ruined the whole thing. It is only another instance that half-confidences between confederates won't pay."

Pigott was delighted with his own sharpness, and laughed to scorn Bertrand's dissent from his theory; "but of course," he added, "I needn't congratulate you. You would never be so base as to deprive your uncle—that kind old uncle, grown grey in the service of his country. It will be necessary to guard the secret most carefully from the unfortunate old man, in case he should insist upon making restitution, or at all events inconvenience himself by doubling your allowance; and any sacrifice would be better than to dissipate his amiable dream that he has disinherited you. You must swear them all to secrecy. Begin with me.

"I am afraid you'll have to pay M'Killop something to keep him quiet; that is a bore. And I'm not sure that I oughtn't to turn an honest penny by the matter myself. You can get the money on post-obits, you know. Your uncle's feelings would not suffer,—he need never know."

" Stop all that nonsense, Pigott, for heaven's sake! I certainly shall claim my birthright— have no fear on that point—though, of course, I shall do what is right by my uncle."

" Write yourself ' of Aberlona,' and let him draw the rents. Yes, that might perhaps miti- gate the shock to his poor old feelings, a little."

" There will be time enough to think of such matters when the investigation is made."

" And what are you going to do now ? "

" Wait to give M'Killop time to divulge it all to me voluntarily."

" Ha! ha! ha! Exactly—give him time for new combinations. You ought to flourish in the next world, Bertrand, for your wisdom is certainly not of this."

During the next few days, while Bertrand's letter to Eila, and Morna's to Mr M'Killop, were on their way to Pau, the two divisions of our *dra- matis personæ*, on either side of the Channel, were, as far as the action of the piece went, pretty much in a state of inaction. There was a lull, for the key to all further action on either side was in the keeping of His Imperial Majesty's Post-Office. We have not seldom had to mourn over the shortcomings of that department in France.

" That, monsieur, would be to effectively degrade the human being to the level of a precise automaton — an inanimate machine," was the ingenious reply of a postmaster in the Gironde to our humble suggestion that a frequent variation of four hours in the time of delivery was inordinate, and might be rectified; but we are bound to say that even the French post-department, in our experience, always seemed to respect the proverb, " that ill news travel fast." The newspaper might be announced as *manqué*, day after day, and the remittance-bearing letter might linger on the road; but we can remember the most perfect punctuality in the arrival of certain other communications which do not, as a rule, sharpen one's appetite for the succeeding meal or two. How does it happen that these are the only exceptions ? Why does not some one write a book of moral speculations on the post-office ? It would suit Victor Hugo, with its sinister mysteries, its thousand epitomes of romance, passion, horror, crime—what you will. He might add another ἀνάγκη to his existing triplet, and christen it "The Post-Office." From such a material he would turn you out a very first-class demon indeed: and we can imagine how it would hoard and grudge; how its baleful eyes would glitter with a malign light over messages of peace, happiness, and love; and how its festering heart would rejoice to project from ill-omened receptacles, with yells of obscene exultation, such despatches as might carry with them grief, terror, shame,—a blow, a stab, and so forth.

Asking pardon for this digression—pardonable, perhaps, as the post-office stops the highway of our story—we repeat that the *dramatis personæ* went on for a few days much as we left them. Eila, at Pau, devoured with secret apprehensions, yet bright as Euphrosyne to all the world about her; Sir Roland apparently enjoying himself very much with his new *protégée* and his old friends; M'Killop in Scotland, haggling for a luck-penny in the matter of Tolmie-Donnochie, but serenely expecting "the happy news;" those at Bournemouth constantly meeting on a pleasant friendly footing, but one of them looking anxiously, between hopes and fears, for the effect of the actual news upon him whose secret she had divulged.

We had forgotten Mrs M'Killop, by the by ; and that lady was carrying a sore and spiteful heart, filled with all uncharity to Eila and Sir Roland, into the *salons* which constituted the poor woman's Paradise of Fools.

Bertrand's letter arrived at last, and as we already know its contents and all that they implied for Eila, we can pretty well imagine the effect it produced upon that young lady. She had not at all blinded herself to the possibility of such a response ; but the contemplation of it had been too bewildering to allow her to provide for the contingency by any reserve plan of action. The letter came, and found her unprepared, and it filled her with consternation. How was she to account for it to her father, who was so set upon the marriage ? how prevent him from calling Bertrand to account ? how therefore escape the full exposure of her conduct ? How was she to baffle the female inquisition of her irrepressible step-mother ? and supply Bertrand with anything like an unassailable reason for his change of purpose ? Last, but not least, how could she satisfy Sir Roland, and prevent him from sifting the matter to the bottom ?

These questions rose before her, clamouring for an instant solution. What was she to do?

No one who had acted as she had acted could have any pride, in the higher sense of the term, to be galled by Bertrand's calm, judicial severity. Her mind was not agitated by any such emotion : any feeling of soreness at having been baffled and defeated, was kept in check by a sort of gambler's sentiment, that, in the game she had been playing without any personal *animus* whatever, the cards had gone against her simply : there was the loss, and to meet it was her business in the mean time. If there was any spite against the adversary, that was not the question of the moment—it would keep. She could postpone that, as well as the pleasure of any practicable revenge, till a future opportunity. Business first, pleasure afterwards. And thus to the business of the moment she was able to bring a mind unclouded with other considerations ; but even that did not seem to help her ; solution after solution presented itself, only to be rejected more or less summarily.

To make a confidante of her step-mother, and so, by flattering her vanity, secure her co-operation and silence ; to prostrate herself before Sir

Roland, and confess, with irresistible tears, that she was tired of Bertrand, and must jilt him— even to hint, perhaps, that another and more venerable image had replaced the idol she felt compelled to shatter; to seize upon the cleanest and most solvent-looking Count from the ranks of the *nunquam non parati* who surrounded her, and solve the difficulty by walking off with him into the hazy regions from which he derived his title : such and suchlike were the only outlets she could discern, and none of them was palatable. She was baffled. Two days passed and found her in the same position.

" It is strange that you have not heard from Bertrand," remarked her step-mother on the second.

" It is very strange," was the serene reply ; but if Count Horneyhoff, or even Baron Hunkers, could, at that moment, have preferred his suit, the odds are that there was a Countess or a Baroness all ready to the hand of either nobleman.

The third day Sir Roland also remarked it : " The dog is coming himself, evidently," he said ; " but it is odd he doesn't even telegraph."

The situation was becoming simply desperate,

and her father might return any day : what was
to be done ?

The strain began to be too much for her, it
was so unremitting. Her nights became sleepless, haunted by the unsolved problem, and by
day she was for ever on the alert, watching every
turn of the conversation, and exercising a providential finésse to divert it from any topic, however remote, that *might* lead to the subject of
Bertrand's silence.   She became afraid to be
with her mother or Sir Roland without the presence of a third party, and to avoid this was
another call upon her watchful ingenuity.   All
this began to tell upon her appearance and manner; and the symptoms of internal dispeace were
legible enough in her pinched features, in the
dark circles round her wearied eyes, and in spasmodic alternations from abstraction to forced
vivacity.

Sir Roland's experienced eye detected this
change, and he pondered deeply over it.   He
had far too much at stake *not* to be anxious till
the marriage was over ; and, being anxious, it
was not unnatural that his own selfish fears
should suggest that something had gone wrong
between Bertrand and Eila.   But he was not the

man to remain in suspense on the subject, or to delay healing measures if they were necessary; and therefore, on the fourth day of Eila's agony, he called and sent up a message inviting her to go out for a walk with him.

Mrs M'Killop was, at the moment, getting unpleasantly close to the fatal subject in conversation, and Eila was glad to make her escape; otherwise she would have declined Sir Roland's invitation. She was obliged, however, to provide for each emergency as it arose, even though the provision was no better than a transfer from the frying-pan to the fire, and *vice versâ.* So she went.

Sir Roland was more than usually affable as they strolled into the park; he was more than usually lively and entertaining; but he watched her narrowly with quick sidelong glances; saw an aggravation of all the symptoms of yesterday; observed that his vivacity (which was tentative) jarred upon her; and that the attempt to carry on an easy conversation with an unconstrained manner, was taxing her powers beyond endurance. He resolved to unriddle the mystery, so he paused abruptly in the conversation, stopped short, looked at her fixedly, and then, as if noticing something amiss for the first time, suddenly cried out—

“God bless my soul! my dear girl, what is the matter? You are looking shockingly ill—pale as death—thin, worn, miserable—what is it?—how have I not noticed it sooner? You have some misery on your mind—tell it to me, my dear child, and perhaps I may be able to help you.”

“It is nothing,” said Eila, in a voice scarcely above a whisper.

“Nothing! come, come, Eila, you can’t deceive me; and why should you? believe me that your happiness is very near my heart.”

Up to a certain point, women are immeasurably superior to men in the sort of game Eila was playing; their finesse is subtler, their self-control more absolute, their power of dissembling infinitely more refined; but, in the language of the turf, they can’t “stay” as men can; they are handicapped with nerves much more heavily than the nobler sex; and, in a protracted trial, the overweighting tells, and they break down. Eila had reached her distance; she had gone so far with unflinching endurance, but she could do no more; the collapse came, and she burst into an hysterical fit of weeping.

Fortunately the park was empty, so that there were no witnesses of the scene. Sir Roland conducted her tenderly to one of the benches, sat down by her, holding her hand in both his, with gentle soothing pressures, but said nothing till the hurricane passed off.

We of the rougher sex cannot comprehend the relief afforded by this "luxury of tears;" but the effect on the female of "a good cry" seems to be about the same as that produced by "a good stiff 'corker' of brandy" on the collapsed nervous system of the male.

Eila's attack was sufficiently violent and genuine while it lasted, but it soon passed off, leaving all her faculties clearer than they had been for days, and, under the circumstances, she gave herself time for reflection, by protracting her formal recovery as long as possible; but as nothing suggested itself to her, better than the old expedient of flight, she "came to" and begged to be taken home at once.

"Very well, my dear," said Sir Roland, "let us go; but I must ask you just one question—

now you are calm. Is it about Bertrand you
are distressing yourself ? ”

“ Please don’t ask me.”

“ Yes, indeed I must ; you have heard from
him ? be frank with me ; I am sure you have
heard from him.”

“ Yes, I have,” said Eila, in desperation.

“ And when is he coming ? ”

“ He is *not* coming.”

“ What ! ” cried Sir Roland ; “ not coming ?
Upon my word he shows mighty little regard for
my convenience ; you told him, I suppose, that it
was my wish, in which you agreed, that the marriage should take place here ? ”

“ Yes, I did.”

“ And what does he suggest ? ”

“ Nothing at all ; he will not marry me at
all.”

“ Almighty heavens ! what do you say ? ”
roared his Excellency ; “ breaks his engagement ? ”

“ Yes.”

Sir Roland, hereupon, quite forgot himself,
and his diplomatic reserve, and fell to apostro-
phising his nephew, in a torrent of “ shocking
bad language,” shaking in the vehemence of his

evil passion. It was clearly the moment for a recurrence of the hysterics ; and they recurred accordingly, the head of the patient dropping on to the shoulder of her companion. The hysterics and this pathetic symptom were, however, for a time, quite lost upon Sir Roland. He put his arm round her waist, indeed, but quite mechanically—the result of an inveterate habit, perhaps ; in other respects he was entirely oblivious of her whose wrongs appeared to excite him so deeply.

Fierce wrath against his nephew — burning, fiery hatred to old M'Killop, and bitter self-reproach at having lent himself to a dishonourable contract—and all for nothing,—these were his first emotions ; and they were expressed in loud incoherent maledictions quite unworthy of an Excellency, in the presence of a lady.

If a dispassionate outsider could have witnessed the tableau, it would certainly have struck him as comical.

A beautiful young lady, weeping and wailing on the shoulder of an elderly satyr, who mechanically fondled her, but was otherwise heedless of her plight, as, with averted head and swollen features, he sat cursing everybody and everything, in a most catholic spirit.

But even Sir Roland's large *repertoire* had a limit, and when he had cursed himself out, more practical reflections recurred.

This was ruin, pure and simple, if it could not be stopped—he saw that; for, as an " honourable man," he could not, of course, purchase M'Killop's silence, even if it was in the market, which seemed doubtful.

But how far the mischief was reparable,—that was the thing to be ascertained, now; and, to ascertain it, he talked right through the hysterics, with the most selfish indifference.

The hysterics accommodatingly paused to let his question be heard, and did not find it necessary to recur.

" What reason does he dare to give for this ? " said Sir Roland.

" He has changed his mind ; he does not care for me ; he does not trust in me."

" How ? "

" I declined, you know," continued Eila, shifting her head to Sir Roland's biceps, so as to bring her eyes into play—" I declined to have anything to say to him, without your sanction."

" You did ?   Well ? "

" This has enraged him ; I fear his temper is

sadly vindictive; and he writes to me, spurning me, Sir Roland—spurning *me*."

"By the lord Harry! he shall eat his words."

"No, no, I beg of you; no. He says, 'Apparently you prefer Sir Roland's good opinion, Sir Roland's affection, to mine; I leave you to him.'"

"Oh, this is some lover's whim, some mere caprice; it must be righted; you have been teasing him, perhaps; but leave him to me—I'll bring him to his senses quick enough. What! sacrifice a beautiful, charming, angelic girl, and himself into the bargain, to his own vile temper! No, no; I won't let him cut his own throat;— no, no."

"Sir Roland, listen to me—I will not have you write to this man! he has insulted me beyond endurance. If he prayed on his knees to me for a century, I would not consent even to look at him; do you understand me?"

"I hear you, my dear child, but I do not understand you. You are over-excited; think no more of it, now. To-morrow we can discuss it coolly."

"I am perfectly cool, Sir Roland; and you must promise me not to write to him."

"Not till you permit me; but do you not love him, then?"

"I detest him;—any feeling I once may have had has been worn out by his childish folly, his outrageous temper, his vanity, and his weakness; he is too boyish. I feel that I could not lean upon such a heart" (and here she nestled closer to Sir Roland's, as if to indicate that it was of a more suitable pattern), "so it is as well as it is; I can't think how a nephew can be so unlike an uncle. Say nothing, please, to anybody about it. I would not have even papa and mamma know how I have been humiliated; you must help me to concoct a story for them; will you not?"

"I am perplexed," stammered Sir Roland; "but I will—I will think it over. You are quite certain that a reconciliation is impossible?"

"Positively; I would never listen to it."

"I am perplexed," repeated his Excellency, hazily: and well he might be; for to concoct a story for M'Killop that would have any saving effect on his own prospects, was a stiffish undertaking. "I am perplexed, but I will speak to you to-morrow. Can we meet at the same hour?"

"Certainly."

"Till then, no more of it; now let us return."
And they went home almost without exchanging
a word.

The burden had, to some extent, fallen from
Eila's shoulders. She had, at least, found and
initiated a policy; she had made a sort of pseudo-
confidant, as against her father and mother, and
she had commanded him to concoct ways and
means of her escape from the dilemma. But if
the burden had been shifted from her shoulders,
it had assuredly transferred itself to those of her
confidant with a very much enhanced weight.

His Excellency staggered under it; he was not
merely perplexed, he was at his wits' end; no
course seemed before him but to walk out of his
worldly possessions and all their direct and in-
direct advantages, and beg " this infernal, hare-
brained, upsetting, romantic noodle of a nephew"
to walk into them; while he settled down, on
a miserable pittance of a half-pension, at some
small Continental town. That was the only
course which he could pursue, according even to
his filmy view of honour. The other alternative
was too broad. To purchase Mr M'Killop—that
was the only other line he could, at first, see;
but that was a naked fraud, and it looked ex-

tremely nasty without any clothing. But, on
continued reflection, M‘Killop was rolling in
money; he was not purchasable; no money
would silence him if he had made up his mind
to speak; so the fraud looked all the nakeder
and uglier for being impracticable. Was there
no other means of circumventing him? M‘Killop's interest was clearly to keep quiet; but he
had shown premonitory symptoms of growing
a conscience; what could check them? if not
money, what then? Was there no other device
that would be as efficacious, and, at the same
time, not be so indecently and vulgarly nude?
Voyons.

That night the Duchess of Esil, Lady Grampington, and a certain French marquis of the old
régime, had to play dummy whist: they waited
for the complementary member of the *partie* till
their noble tempers were sadly exasperated; and,
at last, a message came that he was indisposed.
Sir Roland was, in fact, engaged in playing, with
a spectral adversary, a game of chess, his bad
angel suggesting the moves. The advice of his
monitor must have been effective, and he must
have won; for on rising to go to bed, he muttered, with a not very angelic smile, "That

will checkmate him, and the game *must* be mine."

When Sir Roland had made up his mind to join M'Killop in his scheme and to defraud his nephew, he had amused, though it can scarcely be said that he deceived, any little remnant of a conscience he possessed, by assuring himself that, by one compensation and another, Bertrand would not be materially a loser. Still the resolution had educated him to the idea of a fraud : as a matter of fact, it had done so ; for the juggle of compensation was only a little bit of gilt gingerbread, offered, in a sort of honorary way, as a bribe to a *quasi* moral sense, and more to keep up a respectable fiction than for any other purpose. He had looked fraud deliberately in the face—there was the great fact ; and, though he had covered it up immediately with a flimsy veil, the shock of novelty could never again disturb him on a reperusal of its "hateful mien." To have formed the resolution at all, showed that he was pretty near the bottom of the *facilis descensus;* and it supplied any little impetus that was necessary to tumble him down into the depths, when his self-interest gravitated in the same direction.

His self-interest did now so gravitate unmistakably; and the question of a fraud on his nephew—a pure uncompensated fraud—gave him surprisingly little trouble; the moral difficulties of doing the thing at all, were almost immediately lost sight of in the superior difficulty of inducing M'Killop to co-operate. How that was to be done had occupied his thoughts this evening. The result of his reflections was, that M'Killop's co-operation could only be secured by stratagem; he thought he saw the way to checkmate him, as he had exclaimed; and he made his first move in that direction the next morning, by writing the following letter to Eila :—

"My dear Eila,—I have employed the interval since we parted, in trying to find a solution for your troubles and my own : I couple my own with yours, not only because whatever troubles you distresses me, but because, both by the infamous conduct of my nephew and by my own involuntary agency, I feel, to a certain degree, responsible for the situation in which you find yourself. I said I was perplexed yesterday, and I have had many hours of perplexity since. I have, however, found a solution which would certainly relieve you from your painful position, though, it is more than possible, you may be unwilling to adopt it.

"I have looked at the situation from your point of view and from my own, and, looking at it from yours and through your delicate sensibility, I can see very clearly all from which you recoil.

"The humiliation of a sudden, unexplained desertion; the sympathy and the sneers of society; the indelible brand of slight and rejection; the line your father will take; the publicity he will give to the scandal by instituting a suit; the exposure in court of all your most sacred feelings; the sneering of impertinent counsel over your letters; the jeering of the audience and the press,—I can quite comprehend how you recoil from such an ordeal.

"Now for my solution. I take it for granted that any girl of sensibility would rather underlie the imputation of *having* jilted, than that of having *been* jilted. Well, you must turn the tables on Bertrand; you must jilt him, before it has got wind that he has broken faith with you; in a word, you must marry immediately. The suggestion startles you perhaps, or you think I jest. 'Husbands don't grow like black-berries,' you will say. True; but I don't jest, and, what is more, I see a husband all ready, if you will only take him. 'Who is he?' you ask. Wait a little.

"I have looked at the matter from *my* point of view also, I told you. Very well; and I have said to myself, 'Here is the most charming girl in Christendom, and she has been treated infamously by my scoundrel of a nephew. He has put her in a dreadful position. I am bound to get her out of it, not only because of my affection for her, but because she has been com-promised by my kinsman. She must marry. Good; but she must marry well—into a position and a fortune worthy of her. Clearly so; but she must marry immediately; and how to find a suitable match for her immediately? there is the question. It is difficult, but I am bound to do it.'

"Very well. I offer you, my dear girl, my own fortune and my own position—neither of them altogether despicable. The feeling that I can be of use to you emboldens me to make the offer which your charms, the moment I saw you, sug-gested to my heart. If you will take these offerings, burthened with an old fellow who loves you very dearly—*vous voilà*—you will find your solution, and make me the happiest of men. If you cannot do this, of course you shall have my friendliest services in attempting to find some other means of extrication; though, I confess, this is the only one that presents itself. I think I could make you very happy, and the position in which I should place you would be more suitable to your grace and refinement than is your present home, with the uncongenial society of a step-mother whose vulgarity makes you wince, and whose unkindness to you has often pained me. I have written this rather than said it, so as to give you time for reflection. But let our meeting take place, as arranged, this afternoon, and then you shall give me your answer. Believe me that I await it as eagerly as if I was —what shall we say?—twenty years younger! Let it be ' Yes!' dearest Eila; oh, let it be ' Yes!'

" Yours most affectionately,

" ROLAND CAMERON."

Let us not suppose that, in writing this letter, Sir Roland was not proposing a step that was most uncongenial to him. He abhorred the

marriage tie, and, indeed, had spent a good deal
of his time in practically evincing his contempt
and disregard for it. It suggested to him trouble,
boredom, bondage, and a total revolution in his
habits ; he also felt that he should incur ridicule
—and, in fact, if Eila's antecedent arrangement
got wind, which it certainly would, something
more than ridicule. Still it was his only resource ; it was the only effectual way of shutting
M'Killop's mouth. The alternatives before him
were, Marriage or Ruin ; and as the former was
clearly the minor evil, he adopted it.

Eila's personal attractions were a slight alle-
viation, certainly ; but, after all, only a slight one.

So he wrote the letter, feeling that he was
paying no small price for his preservation.

That which was to be done must be done
promptly, however ; and he despatched the letter
with all haste, and determined to carry out his
plan with the utmost energy. His knowledge of
character gave him considerable hope that his
suit would not be rejected ; but as it was the last
card in his pack, he awaited the result with
much anxiety.

When Eila received the letter she carried it
to her own room for perusal.

Its contents may, or may not, have been un-expected; they certainly were not unwelcome, for "Thank heaven! thank heaven!" were her pious ejaculations when she had read it through; and then, having laid it on her toilette table, she looked in the glass, and murmured to herself, with a pleasant smile, "Lady Cameron!" The marriage was, in fact, not only welcome as a means of extrication, but perfectly so for its own sake. She had no foolish prejudices about inequality of years. To her, marriage was a practical, not a sentimental, question. An elderly husband was even more desirable than a young one, according to her creed, which said, "It is better to be an old man's darling than a young man's slave." So that, if Sir Roland and Bertrand had originally come on the *tapis* together as rivals, Bertrand's chances would certainly have been slender. It would have resolved itself pretty well into a match between *fee-simple* and reversionary interests, and Eila was quite aware that a bird in the hand is worth two in the bush, for she had plenty of proverbial wisdom at command.

In spite of Bertrand, she would thus still have the same fortune and a better position—all at

once, too, without waiting for dead men's shoes.
How that would gall Bertrand! And what
glory to domineer over Mrs M'Killop! what an
extinguisher this would be for her insolence, her
affected superiority, her nonsensical pedigree!
Lady Cameron of Aberlorna would put Mrs
M'Killop of Tolmie-Donnochie in her place, and
keep her there. Then the county neighbours
who had ignored them; — what bliss to snub
them all round as the great lady of the district!
She would turn the tables on *them* with a ven-
geance; and Mr Tainsh's brutality to her, that
would not be forgotten. Tainsh should either
be summarily dismissed from his factorship, or
retained for purposes of persecution.

It was a glorious vista. She rubbed her hands
with delight as she contemplated it, and reflected
on her marvellous escape, and how two days ago
she might have thrown herself to the dogs, and
espoused a Horneyhoff.

Again and again she expressed the devoutest
gratitude to Heaven.

There were minor difficulties to encounter, of
course. Her father might be troublesome; he
was set on the marriage with Bertrand, whom
she was to jilt,—ha! ha!—but Sir Roland must

manage all that. Under the shelter of his name and position, it mattered little to her what her relations thought, or said, or did. Sir Roland would make the details all right; and with such thoughts she tripped out joyously to meet him; and never with a brighter mien, or half so light a heart, had she gone forth to meet her gallant young lover in the summer woods.

> "Ah, that deceit should steal such gentle shapes,
> And with a virtuous visor hide deep vice!"

She arrived first at the rendezvous, and had time to pose herself and study an effective overture before Sir Roland made his appearance.

The *rôle* she should adopt had been a subject of some doubt to her. She had hesitated whether to play Beggar-maid to his Cophetua, or the coy and difficult nymph requiring solicitation and time for thought. But the latter was too hazardous; the time was so short that her art must be no longer than was absolutely necessary; and she decided for a modified reading of the "Beggar-maid." This resolution had scarcely been taken, when the sound of approaching steps warned her to fall into a fit of deep abstraction, from which she did not awake till the fitting moment, when Sir Roland was, so to speak, within range.   Then she looked up with a start, rose quivering, went forward to meet him, with two or three steps of impassioned energy, gave him one long, thrilling glance, and fell upon his bosom.

"Mine, Eila? mine?" cried the old reprobate.

"It is your generosity, and not your love—it cannot be your love—that has prompted you to this," she murmured.

"It is my fervent love, my darling—I swear to it," cried Sir Roland.

"No, no, it is your chivalry that speaks," moaned the Beggar-maid.

"It is my love, which I glory in," shouted King Cophetua. "I will go on my knees to you, and swear it" (he didn't, though), "and beg for a little in return."

"Ah! what heart could refuse love to such noble generosity?"

"Do not talk of generosity; tell me that you believe in my love; tell me that you return it a little; tell me that you accept me, and then I shall be happy."

"I do,—I do,—all—all!"

"Then I am happy," cried Sir Roland; and nothing further of a sentimental nature occurring to him to say at the moment, he set to work and kissed his *fiancée* in a very business-like way, conducting her drooping form, with a "long-drawn-out sweetness" of slow progression, back to the seat from which she had arisen. It was a loathly sight.

The interview between this well-matched pair was a long one. The main question—that of the marriage — was carried, as we have seen, *nem. con.;* but when it got into committee, there was a good deal of debate and difficulty in adjusting some of the details. A business-like spirit being displayed on both sides, however, and an honest desire to effect a settlement, all difficulties were, at length, removed, and the session closed with the sentimental formalities which had marked its opening. Let us leave the romantic lovers for a little to themselves.

CHAPTER XXXVIII.

IT had been arranged that Morna should seize the opportunity of M'Killop's return to Pau to rejoin her family, under his escort; and, about ten days after her first meeting with Bertrand, she received her step-father's summons to meet him in London on the following day.

During these ten days, Bertrand had been as good as his word, and called upon Morna, who had undoubtedly fulfilled her part of the engagement, by being very glad to see him. The experiment, indeed, was found so agreeable by both, that it was repeated; and it became a daily occurrence that they should meet somehow or other, either by appointment, or by that sort of accident which is so apt to bring people together, when they desire to meet. But their meetings were not restricted by the usual limits of a formal call, or a chance greeting in the market-place; their interviews were long, and even confidential. We know that they had established a confidence on their first meeting; and one confidence begets another. Love is a subject on which every patient desires communion of the sort (most of us have suffered, probably, from the fact), whether it be to laud the object of his passion, or to denounce her perfidy—to dilate on the beauty of the flower, or to mourn over its broken stem and blackened leaves.

Morna very soon became the receiver of Bertrand's tale of wrong.

Her frank sympathy soon thawed his reserve, and even broke down the *quasi* generous pride which, at first, made him unwilling to paint, in its true colours, the conduct of her who had wronged him. But sympathy is a powerful engine; and it opened up to Morna all the sorrows of Bertrand's lacerated heart; and for hours he would dilate upon them, with that eloquence which egotism lends to all mankind.

Would male sympathy have stood the test of such an infliction? And, even if it had, would it have been resorted to with equal gusto?

Certainly not. The subject is pre-eminently suited to a female confidante; and, when she is young and pretty, her sympathy has a double action, for while it opens up the wound, it pours into it a subtle and consolatory balsam.

But is a female confidante proof against the boredom of her office? Is the subject of such abstract interest as to rivet her attention and her sympathy, be the confider who and what he may?

Without deciding on the general question, it is quite certain that Morna was not bored at all, that her attention and her sympathy were inexhaustible, and that, in fact, these interviews, at which the conversation grew daily less and less lugubrious, became to her daily more and more delightful.

There is a saying that every woman delights in the dispraise and discredit of every other woman—a dreadful saying, but worthy, it is to be feared, of some little acceptation.

Still Morna was rather an exceptional woman; and it certainly was not exclusively from this source, that the interviews carried delight to her heart.

There was no doubt that her beautiful Prince had reappeared. She had but two associations connected with him—fairy-land and a malign enchantress. But the spells of the latter had been so far broken, and was it therefore wonderful that again around her should begin to loom some gladsome visions of the dazzling realm ?

As for the beautiful Prince himself, the relief of talking over all his feelings and experiences unchecked by the dread of male sneers, had a wonderfully beneficial effect upon his mind and body; and Pigott observed that, by the time Morna's stay came to a close, he was able to forget, not only his illness, but its cause, for hours, if not days, together. The cheerfulness of other times came back to him ; he interested himself about the question of his rights, and constantly discussed the subject with his practical friend—totally abandoning the *laissez-aller* tone of the broken-hearted lover, to whom the smiles and the frowns of Fortune are alike indifferent. Pigott, of course, rejoiced at his friend's restoration, though he took his own view of what was likely to be another result of the treatment which had produced it; and his reflections took some such shape as this—" When a young gentleman, recently recovered from a bad attack of being jilted, sits, hour after hour, in romantic spots by the sea, and pours his griefs into the sympathising ear of a handsome young lady, who, moreover, has lately been the means of his hearing 'something greatly to his advantage,' what should we consider a not unlikely result of their confidential intercourse? Why, a discovery on the part of the gentleman that his griefs have ceased to be griefs at all, when so sweetly shared, and an admission on that of the lady, that she is not unwilling to be installed permanently in the office of consoler. No doubt about it; the ass will be in for another fit, as sure as fate; but, thank heaven! he'll be ashamed to say anything about the subject to me for a long time, and I'm not likely to open it."

Notwithstanding Pigott's prophecy, Bertrand and Morna separated without any catastrophe of the sort. No doubt they parted with mutual regret; and it might have gratified the young lady in many ways, as it flattered the prophet's sense of his own acuteness, to observe what a blank her departure made for Bertrand; how he fretted and chafed, and abused Bournemouth; how he swore he would leave it every hour of the day, and how eventually he did so on the third day, returning to his regiment with a fort-night's leave unexpired.

Mr M'Killop had rather hurried over his business in Scotland, so as to get back at the earliest possible moment to Pau, and bring the grand scheme of the marriage to a conclusion. It may be well to explain that he was entirely ignorant of any hitch in the matter ; and as Mrs M'Killop was equally in the dark, her letters could not enlighten him. Eila, as we know, was not likely to supply the information, and Morna had not opened the subject to him, because she supposed the intelligence must have reached him from Pau, and was unwilling to deprive him of the opportunity of taking the initiative as to declaring Bertrand's rights.

Thus it came about that when Mr M'Killop met his step-daughter in London, he was still looking upon the marriage as certain and imminent ; and the only trouble on his mind connected with the business, was the necessity of satisfying her, after the marriage, that there was an *entente cordiale* between uncle and nephew, by which the latter had agreed to suspend his rights in favour of the former, for solid considerations. To do this it would be necessary that Sir Roland should settle an unusually handsome allowance on the young couple ; something, in fact, so large as to satisfy Morna that it was given by way of compromise ; and the problem was how to induce Sir Roland to do this, without letting him know that the secret was shared by a third person. He was sanguine, however, that this could be arranged somehow, and met Morna with a cheerfulness that was not altogether assumed. That cheerfulness, it may well be supposed, did not survive their meeting many minutes.

" Well, Morna," cried Mr M'Killop, gaily, " here we are, all hasting to the wedding! Have you got your finery ready ? "

" No," said Morna, much puzzled ; " it isn't necessary."

" Ah !" M'Killop rattled on, " a great mistake that—a great mistake ; although it may be a quiet wedding, and abroad, and so on, still a wedding *is* a wedding—the spinster's opportunity, you know, ha! ha! We must be fine, Morna, we must be fine ; and it isn't too late. We've got Paris between us and Pau ; and we'll just see if Paris, and you, and I, and my purse, between us, can't turn them out a creditable bridesmaid. We'll astonish your mother. I suppose the happy man is there, by this time ?"

" I don't the least understand what you are talking about, Mr M'Killop. It is impossible that you don't know the marriage is broken off ? "

" *Was* broken off, my dear, of course—postponed, at least ; but, bless me, didn't you get my letter from Pau ? "

" I did."

" Well."

" But, since that, surely you know that everything is at an end ? "

" You're dreaming, girl."

" No, indeed, I am not."

" Well, if a marriage is broken off, it seems likely that the bride's father should be aware of it."

" So it does ; but if the bridegroom tells you he is not going to be a bridegroom, it seems still more likely that he ought to know."

" What bridegroom ? What nonsensical stuff is this you have got hold of ? "

" Mr Cameron told me, with his own lips, that his marriage is broken off."

" When ? "

" No later than yesterday."

" But he is at Pau."

" No ; he is at Bournemouth ; I left him there."

There is no rest for the wicked. Destiny seemed to be forcing Mr M'Killop to act *like* an honest man, and tell the truth at last. It was desperately hard upon him. " For all his pains, poor man !—for all his pains," the rope by which he was attempting to bind Honesty, Fraud, and Self-interest together, seemed for ever to crumble like True Thomas's ropes of " the sifted sand."

But it would not do to collapse while there was a chance left; and, after a painful pause, he spoke again.

" Who is to blame ? "

" Eila," replied Morna, very decidedly.

" What ? do you tell me that she jilted him ? "

" In a certain way she undoubtedly did. She has treated him ill."

" And he resents it ? "

" He does."

" The girl must be mad; but I'll bring her to her senses quickly enough. She shall eat humble-pie ; she shall apologise."

" I don't think your interference can possibly do any good."

" Oh, can't it ? wait till you see ; I'll stake

my reputation that the marriage comes off.
What were her reasons?"

" She has not written to me; you must wait
and hear her story. I am sure she would not
like me to discuss her affairs with you; pray do
not press me to do so."

"Yes; and if she thinks she is going to throw
away a marriage like that, for some silly tantrum,
she is much mistaken; I'll give her twenty-four
hours for reflection, and then——"

M'Killop did not mention his ultimatum, but
as he understood the hitch to be upon his
daughter's side, he appeared satisfied that the
ultimatum would be effective.

" There is another subject I wish to speak
about," said Morna.

" What is it?"

" I don't wish to be importunate, but, now the
marriage is broken off, you will arrange about—
about—the rights—the Cameron property, will
you not?"

" Good heavens!" roared M'Killop, " the
marriage is *not* broken off. • I tell you the
marriage will come off within the month.
Leave me to do the right thing at the right
time——"

" But if I am right——"

" Who are you, to teach me my duty ? Hold your tongue."

And Morna did so, in the mean time, resolved to let it loose freely enough, if, after M‘Killop had satisfied himself at Pau that the marriage was really off, he did not speak out at once.

The journey, as may be imagined, was tedious and cheerless enough. The silence was almost unbroken between them all the way. They stopped one night in Paris, where M‘Killop's gay proposal as to a *trousseau* was not reverted to—and one night in Bourdeaux, reaching Pau on the third afternoon—M‘Killop, full of impatience to clear matters up with his daughter, and Morna with such a prospect of domestic discord and unhappiness before her, as to obscure pretty effectually for her the glories of the grand Pyrenean panorama, which she saw for the first time. When the travellers reached their destination, they found Mrs M‘Killop at home, seated alone in her brilliant *salon*. It was the hour when she had a right to expect that the nobility and gentry might pay their respects, and she was posed for their reception, with a certain imperial pomp of aspect, and many a glittering circumstance of personal decoration.

Every day developed some new splendour in this costly woman. She believed herself to be a Queen of the fashion, and had so far succeeded in providing herself with a suitable wardrobe and regalia, that, when in *grande tenue*, her appearance indifferently suggested the ideas of Solomon in all his glory, and of a Christmas-tree in full illumination.

The appointments of her drawing-room were in keeping with her quality of sovereign, and symbolised the character of the subjects over whom she believed herself to reign ; for the great red woman wallowed in a higgledy-piggledy litter of gorgeous frippery.

Even her husband, with all his preoccupation, did not fail to note the surprising progress achieved during his short absence; and to Morna, who had known her only in the simpler if more barbaric efflorescence of tartan and cairngorm, the effect was tremendous.

With as much affection as was compatible with lofty station, Mrs M'Killop greeted her daughter, descending, as it were, two steps of the throne, and offering her ruby cheek; restricting her husband, however, to a momentary handlement of two sausage-like fingers.

" I made no doubt," she said, sinking back on her throne—" I made no doubt, when the door opened, that it was General Chuffey" (the General was an American warrior, whose martial heels had distinguished themselves in several trying stampedes), " or Count Puffendart; they were both to pay their *devours* this afternoon."

" I hope you won't have company this afternoon," said M'Killop.

" Oh, there will be company—they come in flocks; but, for once, if you insist, I can disappoint them; I can let the *conserge* say I am *sortee*."

" Please do so; we have a good deal to talk about."

" Ah! *vraimong?* *Swaw dong;*" and she bade him ring the bell, and sentence of exclusion was recorded against the *beau monde*.

" And where is Eila?" asked her father.

" Aw! don't ask me; I know nothing about *her*," said the dame, with a toss.

" What do you mean? Is she well?"

" I preshoom she is well, but I protest it is only guess-work—I never see her."

“ I don’t understand you.”

“ And I don’t understand *her ;* her conduct is peculiar; she avoids me : she is out half the day, and when she is in, she keeps to her own room ; and if I speak to her, she either don’t answer me at all, or with sauce. I am glad you are come back, M‘Killop. The girl is too much for my nervous system. I hope you are going to arrange for the marriage at once. Where is the man ? Have you not brought him ? ”

“ No, I am rather puzzled about affairs. Morna has some story that Eila and Bertrand have had a split ; do you know anything of it ? ”

“ *Mwaw?* I neither know nor care anything about her and her affairs.”

“ Yes, but I insist that you shall both know and care, Mrs M‘Killop,” retorted her husband, in a dangerous voice ; “ there is a quarrel between them, and you must know the rights of it : none of your airs, madam ; keep them for your cursed Counts, and tell me what you know, at once.”

“ I tell you, Mr M‘Killop, that I know nothing about her affairs,” replied the lady, sulkily ; “ and if there is a quarrel she has not told me of it. Ask herself ; ring ; send for her ; not that she will be at home.”

“ Not at home ? where is she, then ? ”

“ How can I tell ? ”

“ It is your duty to know, madam ; is it the custom for mothers or step-mothers to let their girls go about alone in a place like this ? ”

“ Not alone ; she will not be alone ; that you may depend upon.”

“ Who is she with, then ? ”

“ Who ? who but that odious old reprobate ? ”

“ Whom do you mean ? ”

“ Her uncle, that-is-to-be, of course.”

“ Ah ! *they* have not quarrelled, then ? There --what do you say to that, Morna ? ”

“ Quarrelled ? ” cried Mrs M‘Killop, “ they are as thick as thieves ; he is a vile creature of a terrible *movy tong*—quite the *burgess*, Horneyhoff says.”

“ Horneyhoff be hanged ! ” cried M‘Killop.

“ And hasn’t even the manners to call upon me ; of course he hasn’t the *entrée* to our set ; still he must know that he is entitled to pay his respects to me, under the circumstances ; but he doesn’t ; no, he is too much taken up toadying that vulgar Duchess, and that Marchioness— persons of no origin. Baron Hunkers says he could not countenance them in his own country, where the *Hot Knoblesse* are particular about pedigree; so he declines to be mixed up with them here; and Gratte-la-nuque calls one the *Bambeeny*, and the other *Boof Gras*, which is as much as to say that they are no better than they should be. Gratte-la-nuque has a way of hitting the nail on the head—and——"

"For God's sake, woman, stop this nonsense! when is Eila likely to be in?"

"You may ask the *conserge*," said Mrs M'Killop, in a pet. But M'Killop was not called upon to make the exertion, for at this moment the door opened, and in walked the young lady in question, followed by Sir Roland.

On seeing her father and Morna she gave a little start of astonishment; and, by the expression of her face, the surprise was genuine, and not agreeable. She looked hurriedly and inquiringly round to her companion, who replied by a scarcely perceptible shrug, which said to her, "The play has to be played with a different company, but play it out."

"My dear papa, what a surprise! back at last! and Morna too!" she exclaimed, treating both of them to elaborate embraces; while Mrs M'Killop, who had risen, returned Sir Roland's bow with a sort of stamp, and stood glowering at him like a cow who sees a dog enter her paddock, and deliberates upon the simplest method of tossing him.

"Delighted to see you again, Sir Roland," said M'Killop. "I've made all haste back, you see."

"Glad to see you back again, Mr M'Killop," replied his Excellency; and they shook hands with the hearty cordiality of men who hate and distrust each other.

"Couldn't keep impatient lovers waiting, you know, ha! ha! Have you heard from Bertrand?"

"I have not," said Sir Roland, with a kind of desperate emphasis, and a come-one-come-all expression on his bad face.

"No? ah! well, Eila, you can tell me of him, surely?"

"Did you not see him in England?" said Eila.

"No, I didn't."

"Nor hear from him?"

"Not a line."

"Ah! I daresay he was ashamed to write to you, and no wonder."

“Why, what's the matter? what has he done?”

“You may well ask that.”

“Then I do ask it. I've heard some whisper of a quarrel between you two; but, let me tell you, that after all the trouble we've had, we're not going to allow you to toss over a fine young man for some idle whimsy of a lover's quarrel; you'll just please to make it up at once;” and he looked at Sir Roland for sympathy and encouragement, but saw neither in the horny eyes of his Excellency.

“Ha! ha! ha! ha! ha! ha!” laughed Eila, loud and clear.

“This is not seemly,” said M‘Killop.

“The manners of a *Grizet!*” snorted Mrs M‘Killop.

“Ha! ha! ha!” laughed Eila, again; “tell them, Sir Roland; tell these good people, or I shall die of laughing.”

“Hush, Eila!” said his Excellency.

“Who do you call ‘people,’ you minx?” cried Mrs M‘Killop.

“Hold your tongue, Mrs M‘Killop,” said her husband.

“Ha! ha! ha!” laughed Eila.

“ Sir Roland, explain all this ; I don’t think it can be a joke to *us*, that the marriage should be run through in this way,” said M‘Killop.

“ Well, Mr M‘Killop,” said Sir Roland, fastening his eyes on the centre button of M‘Killop’s waistcoat ; “ Bertrand has turned out shockingly ; he’s a thorough bad one ; instead of appreciating your daughter’s dutiful and proper conduct, in suspending correspondence till my sanction was obtained to the marriage, he has resented it in the language of a bargee—replied to her last letter with coarse and horrible insults, and scouted the bare idea of a marriage between her and himself.　Not content with insulting her, he has dragged you into his infamous letter, and covered you with abusive epithets, unfit for a lady’s eye or ear.　As for myself, his language about me is such that I am compelled to disown him for ever.”

It was odd how Sir Roland seemed to forget Eila’s sensitiveness as to being jilted, and surprising the equanimity with which she listened to the story of her humiliation.

M‘Killop could only stare in bewilderment at the speaker.

There was a dead silence for a few seconds ;

during which Morna came forward as if she was about to speak; but Eila anticipated her, crying out, "Go on, Sir Roland; go on."

"I am going on, my dear, immediately. Very well, Mr M'Killop, I found your daughter smarting under this indignity—grievously smarting, I may say, intensely smarting; in fact, smarting to such an extent that, ahem!—I scarcely know how to express myself;" and he paused again.

"Very well, if you can't speak out, Sir Roland, I will," cried Eila, impatiently, as she rose and came into the centre of the room; "and now," she said, making a mocking curtsey to Mrs M'Killop, "let me introduce you to Lady Cameron, of Aberlorna! Papa, kiss her ladyship," and she turned round to present her cheek to M'Killop, who, however, staggered back against the chimney-piece, with outstretched arms repelling her, his eyes glaring wide open, his lips apart, and his face as white as the marble he leant against.

"Yes," said Sir Roland, rising and regaining his fluency; "I found her in this aggrieved, outraged state, and the victim of my kinsman; I said to myself, 'It is my duty to make reparation;' and, as I loved her very dearly besides, I offered to do what I could to console her for the rest of my days, if she would become my wife. She agreed to make me happy. It was with the deepest pain that we were obliged to hasten the ceremony, and allow it to take place without your presence or consent even; but that was unavoidable. I have been hourly expecting a telegram from the colonial office which might send me back to my government at a day's notice; so, as delay was impossible, we were married this forenoon; and now, I hope you will forgive this, and accept a rather ancient son-in-law." He held out his hand with a feeble attempt at a laugh.

Every point—bow, ribbon, ringlet, and pendicular gewgaw on Mrs M'Killop's person—was meanwhile vibrating with excitement, wrath, surprise, and venomous spite.

"Married!" she exclaimed; "married! like beggars under a hedge! she shall never enter *my* house again, or I hers. Pollution!"

"Ha! ha! ha!" laughed her ladyship, cheerily. " Dear old creature! I knew you would be amusing; but try something fresher than the fox and the grapes; do now—quick; it's your last chance, ha! ha! ha!"

M'Killop stared at Sir Roland's hand for a moment, and then roared out like a bull, "Never!"

"What?" said Sir Roland, "you don't know how the dog abused you, or you would not side with him; he is a common blackguard."

"That is false," said Morna, stepping forward; "the whole story is false from beginning to end. Mr M'Killop, Eila has deceived you; Mr Cameron is not to blame; and this man's story is a lie."

"What a pity he can't hear you! you might have a chance, now I don't require him," sneered Eila.

"I don't care for your sneers; I know how you treated him, and told him lies, and told your father lies, and told this old man lies too, probably; and you have taught him the art, if he required to learn it, for he is telling the vilest lies now about his nephew, and there is not a word of truth between you."

"Pickpockets!" ejaculated Mrs M'Killop.

"Don't hold out your hand to me, sir," repeated M'Killop; "I have done with you; and you, Eila, shall be no daughter of mine, any more."

" Very well, Mr M‘Killop," said Eila, " as you please ; it is just as well, perhaps ; for indeed it relieves me from a difficulty. I could not have shut the door on my own father, and, of course, your coming would have been awkward when we had people with us ; as for these women, their manners would have vulgarised the servants' hall, where they must have waited while you were with me. It is all just as well as it is. Come along, Roland."

" Hush, Eila," said Sir Roland ; " no, no ; you must not speak so unbecomingly to your father. Mr M‘Killop, I hope you will consider our mutual position, and even if we are not to have intercourse——"

" Not another word, sir. Lady Cameron, you seem to be pleased with your new title. It is fortunate. Make the most of it, for it is about all you are likely to gain by your marriage."

" Hush, hush, hush ! Mr M‘Killop ; I beg you to reflect," cried Sir Roland, with vehemence.

" I have reflected, and I am going to let this young lady know her true position. You have married, Lady Cameron, a man old enough to be your grandfather—*that* you can see for yourself; without much character—*that* you may have guessed; and,—what you certainly do *not* know, or you would not be Lady Cameron,—he is without a penny of fortune."

"Ha! ha! I daresay Aberlorna will do very well, without money," laughed Eila.

"Very well for its real owner; but, unfortunately for you, it don't belong to your husband."

"Indeed! and, pray, whose is it, then?" sneered her ladyship.

"It belongs to Mr Bertrand Cameron."

"You are in your dotage."

"Very well; but, what is more, your husband knows that I state what is the fact."

"Sir Roland!" exclaimed Eila, looking round, in surprise at his silence; and the face she looked upon told her at once that there was something in the story.

"Sir Roland!" she almost screamed, "speak —tell me—what does he mean? is this true, or is he mad?"

"No," said Sir Roland, "I don't think he is mad, but he is a thief, a felon, and a convict; probably he believes what he is saying. He stole a will, it seems, ages ago, when engaged in some other little business connected with his then profession of burglar, and he believes this will to set aside my inheritance, but I don't share the belief—that's all."

"You forget, Sir Roland—you forget a certain document signed by you, compounding to be allowed to retain possession of this said inheritance, for such and such considerations, compensating the rightful, though unconscious, owner, in the mean time, and securing his rights to him after your death ;—you forget that. You would scarcely have made such a contract if you had doubted the validity of the will. But I am not going to argue the matter; the documents shall be despatched to Scotland to-night, and the law shall take its course. I would not give you a *sou* for what you are likely to get out of Aber-lorna for the rest of your life, except as a gratuity. So, Lady Cameron, you see your position."

"I don't; I'm all bewildered," stammered Eila ; and indeed the other ladies seemed to share her feelings. "Do you say my father stole a will?"

"He did, unquestionably."

"Knock him down, Mr M'Killop! knock him down with the poker!" cried Mrs M'Killop.

"My father a thief!" ejaculated Eila.

" And your husband a swindler, my lady," said her father.

" M‘Killop, do you stand still and hear that wretch say you robbed a will?" cried Mrs M‘Killop.

" I do."

" If you have not the spirit, I will knock him down myself!" and she began to clear for action, looking physically quite equal to the task.

" No," said M‘Killop, " he speaks the truth. I abstracted a will—accidentally."

" And got sent to Botany Bay by the merest accident in the world," added Sir Roland.

" What !" yelled Mrs M‘Killop, " was he a convict ?"

" An innocent convict, Elizabeth. Listen, I will tell you the story."

But Mrs M‘Killop would none of his explanations. She roared, and screamed, and howled, and bellowed, so that passers-by might have imagined that several tigers were being fed on the premises. She brandished her brawny arms, pointed with her fingers in the faces of her husband and Sir Roland, hissed like a snake, banned them by all her gods, invoked her guttural ancestors, crying out that she would have nothing to

do with jail-birds, and forgers, and murderers—
not she. Finally, after going on like a Fury
and a Mænad, she banged out of the room, calling
upon Morna to come forth from the den of thieves,
if she would escape a long catalogue of calamities,
moral and physical, winding up with jail-fever.

And Morna followed her; but before she went
she walked up to M'Killop, and held out her
hand. "Whatever you may have done before,
you have behaved as an honest man at last,—
and better late than never."

Who can tell how much M'Killop's heroic
achievement was due to her cognisance of the
secret? But she never suspected this.

"Thank you, Morna," said her step-father.
"I would like to tell you my story some day;
meantime don't think too hardly of me. I have
shaken off the last fetters of dishonesty to-day,
at the sacrifice of all my prospects. Virtually I
have banished myself for life; for, even if the
law does not pursue me, society will shun me.
So all my dreams are over; and the place I have
just bought with so much pride may go to the
market again. But my dreams were haunted,
and all my satisfaction would have been poisoned.
I knew it—I knew it; but—ah! well, I have a

clear path before me now. God keep me in it!"

It is quite possible that the man believed himself that he had acted as he had done, from a sudden pure conversion to honesty; and indeed it is not for us to say that he would not have so acted, even if Morna's cognisance had not made any other course impossible.

"Good-bye, Morna. And now, Sir Roland and Lady Cameron, I suppose you have nothing more to say?"

"If my husband is a swindler, I am not going to stay with him," cried Eila.

"Take my word for it, he is a swindler," said her father.

"Then I will stay with you."

"Excuse me, but I am a robber and a convict."

"Still you are my father, and you repent. My duty is by your side. Your daughter will not forsake you."

"I see it is a choice between a penniless swindler and an affluent burglar. But I could not countenance the separation of two people united by so sacred a tie. Go with your husband, girl—go along and make the best of him. He is bound to support you, and I am not."

"If I can find any means of getting you a hot punishment, you infernal gallows-bird, I shall adopt them," snarled Sir Roland.

"Do your worst, you silly old man, and your autograph in my possession will provide something similar for yourself. Go along with you."

And the happy couple sneaked out of the room and out of the house, leaving the "gallows-bird" alone on the stricken field, but certainly not without some of the honours of war.

He sat down dreamily on Mrs M'Killop's vacant throne, and sank into a profound reverie. Since his original lapse, in the stealing of the papers, he had been honest in all his dealings, with this single exception of Bertrand's rights— a trifling exception, he had flattered himself, in which strict honesty was but suspended and not violated—an exception with so many extenuating conditions and specious disguises as scarcely to be an exception, but which would not stand the crucial test to which it was now exposed. He had been in the habit of saying to himself, "I don't make a farthing by the postponement of the lad's rights—not a copper;" and this was an unction which he had constantly applied to his conscience; but now, with a vision cleared of the films of self-interest, he frankly recognised the quackery. He reviewed, with poignant regret, if not contrition, the hopes which his honest toil had striven to realise ; he saw that the efforts of his life had been neutralised by this one divergence from the right line—trifling and venial as he had taught himself to regard it ; and he bitterly deciphered everywhere upon the ruins of his career an inscription whose words of wisdom would have saved it, clearly seen in time, " Honesty is the best policy." It was now too late to rescue much material advantage from the wreck; but inasmuch as it is never too late to mend, it was not too late to secure higher advantages still, for—

> " Men may rise, by stepping-stones
> Of their dead selves, to nobler things."

Engaged, it may be, with some such reflection, his wife and her dramatic departure had altogether escaped his thoughts, and nothing less than her own personal reappearance recalled them. This took place about half an hour after her exit; when the door was partially opened, and the upper part of Mrs M'Killop's body, bonneted and shawled, cautiously displayed itself in the aperture. M'Killop was so immersed in thought that he did not at first observe her, and she was obliged to attract his attention.

“Ahem! ahem!”

M‘Killop looked round, and rose to his feet.

“Don’t come near me,” cried his wife, partially withdrawing her body; “don’t come near me, Barabbas!”

“I have no wish to do so,” said M‘Killop, quietly, “but, before acting as you have done, you ought to have heard my story. Will you listen to me now?”

“Not a word; you have confessed yourself a gallery-slave—that is enough for me.”

“I know you married me for money alone, Elizabeth, but still, if you have any sense of justice or consideration——”

“Justice! justice to you! consideration for you! a man who has entrapped me, a lady of birth and blood, into marrying a vile rogue—a bread-and-water thief, covered with chains and—and straw! I wonder my ancestors can rest in their graves; I wonder Grant can lie at peace on his battle-field; I——”

“You’re certainly making noise enough to disturb them; but, look you, I won’t have it. If

you will not listen to my explanation, neither will
I to your abuse. What brings you here, woman,
if you have nothing more to the purpose to say?
If you have, say it at once ; if not, you shall not
remain here." He turned towards her fiercely,
as he spoke, and his air and gesture warned her
to come to the practical object of her visit at once.

"You have done me a deadly wrong, M'Killop,"
she said, in a quieter tone, "and you are bound
to repair it as well as you can. I am entitled to
a jointure of twelve hundred a-year ; where is
that to come from, pray, if your property is confiscated ? "

" Where, indeed ? " said M'Killop.

"Now, if you have any manhood left in you,
before you are seized, you will write at once and
secure as much as you can and pay it over
to me."

" Ah ! that would be to defraud justice," said
M'Killop, drily.

"Defraud justice, forsooth ! and, pray, what
is justice compared to the widow and the father-
less ? "

" Ha ! ha !" laughed M'Killop. " It is the
convict's wife who is speaking."

"No, sir, it is not the convict's wife—I call myself 'Mrs Grant' from this hour."

"Very well, Mrs Grant, if you are not my wife I am not bound to keep you; if you desert me, Mrs Grant—don't you see?"

"Desert you? Would you have me go to jail with you?"

"Heaven forbid, or anywhere else. But no more of this; I am not bound to support you separately, but I will do so rather than have you with me, for you are of the sort that will soon get over anything, and fly back to money—dirty though it be. My property will not be confiscated; don't be uneasy, you shall have your jointure."

"Paid quarterly in advance, and beginning to-night."

"Very well."

"Write the cheque."

"Here are notes."

Mrs M'Killop entered the room briskly, and received them.

"Ah!" said M'Killop, "what a thing money is, to be sure! it brings you like a lamb into the robber's den, and you have no scruple about touching the accursed thing.   Smell the notes ; is there no taint of jail-fever on them ?   Now, if I offered you three hundred more, you would sit quietly down and listen to my explanation."

"Don't insult me, fellow."

"No, no, Mrs Grant, I won't *tempt* you. Now, go away, and let these excellent ancestors of yours get back to their tombs."

She lingered.

" Well, what is it ? " said M'Killop.

" Just this," she said : " before the police come, you had better send me over these things—ornaments and so forth—to the hotel.   Marie will show you the things."

"Very well, very well," and she departed, but came back again immediately, remarking, " On second thoughts, I'll take the parrot with me," and straightway marched off with it, the bird appropriately screaming, " Au voleur !—au voleur ! " in his gilded cage.

M'Killop gave a shrug and a short laugh ; then opened a bureau, and began to write ; and for hours he was so occupied,—writing rapidly, sheet after sheet, and finally enclosing the result, with certain other documents, in two large envel-

opes, which he carefully sealed and addressed,
one to Mr Tainsh, and the other to Bertrand.
When it was all over—the story of his life told
—the secret divulged—the act of justice done at
last—he gave a long sigh, and his head sank
wearily on the desk, in front of him.

CHAPTER XXXIX.

"Do you really think this will can turn you out of Aberlorna?" was Eila's first question to Sir Roland, when they got outside the house.

"Not a doubt of it; it was always suspected to be my father's intention to dispose of the property in that way."

"And what am I to do?"

"Well, really that hadn't occurred to me; I was selfish enough to be thinking of myself."

"Why did you marry me?"

"Now! now! now! a girl of your acuteness can scarcely require to ask such a question."

"It can't have been for love—that's evident."

"Your perceptions are brightening."

"And I shall have no money?"

"That's the most infernal part of it all."

"What a wicked man you must be!"

"Some people have said so before."

“ I have been made a victim of ; I have been
cheated and deceived.”

“ Blame yourself first, then your father—me
last and least of all : it’s a devilish deal harder
for me than you, my lady. Here am I come
from eight thousand to eight hundred a-year in
one day ; and am saddled with a wife into the
bargain ? ”

“ We can’t live on eight hundred a-year.”

“ I never tried yet.”

“ I shall leave you.”

“ Let us have our wedding dinner, first ; it is
ordered, so we’ll have to pay for it, and it’s a
good one.”

“ Wretch !   I tell you I shall leave you,” said
Eila, stopping and stamping on the ground.

“ My dear creature, the vehemence is quite
uncalled for ; I could not thwart the inclination
of one I love so dearly, for an instant. I only
ventured to offer you a little refreshment before
starting. Does your ladyship propose to make a
long journey this evening ? ”

“ I — oh, miserable ! miserable ! I am all
alone ! ” and the wretched girl burst into a
paroxysm of weeping.

"Don't make a scene in the street, you little fool," said the gallant bridegroom ; and, putting her arm in his, he conducted her rapidly to the hotel—her tears and sobs moving the passers-by to wonder and compassion, and calling forth a few not very balmy curses from her conductor. Nemesis had got her at last, and the hymeneal torch was her instrument of torture.

Towards midnight, Mrs M'Killop and her daughter were still sitting together in their *salon* at the hotel ; for Mrs M'Killop had to ventilate her wrongs ; and she had done it with that prolixity, and that amount of genealogical digression, which was natural to her ; when Marie, the *fille de chambre* of the *appartement* on the terrace, burst into the room, " Oh, madame ! " she exclaimed, " quick, quick ! Monsieur is no more ! "

" What does she say, Morna ? " said Mrs M'Killop, whose knowledge of French was imperfect.

" Monsieur no more, Marie ! what do you mean ? " said Morna.

" That which I have said ; he lies on the floor a dead man ; and, my God, what a pallor ! "

" Mr M'Killop dead, mamma ! Quick, let us

run ; you can follow me ! " and she was off, without bonnet or shawl, the little French maid trotting by her side.

As they went along, she bethought herself, and said, " A doctor, Marie ! run and fetch one."

" The doctor is already with monsieur," said Marie.

" And you are sure he is dead ? "

" One might by hazard be able to say that he yet breathes, *mais très, très peu*," replied the girl, reducing the interest of her news with manifest reluctance, after her kind.

In a few seconds they were at the house.

" No, mademoiselle, certainly not dead," said the doctor, in answer to Morna's rapid inquiries ; " nor even dying. It has been a severe shock ; but with skill and care, monsieur will do very well. Skill, care, and time—*voilà tout*."

" Can I see him ? "

" Undoubtedly ; but mademoiselle is the daughter of the sufferer ? "

" His step-daughter."

" That is equal. Mademoiselle must prepare herself to sustain a painful surprise. The appearance of this poor gentleman has experienced a

change in which there is a certain mournfulness."

" I will go in."

" Monsieur will not have the happiness to
appreciate the graceful tribute which mademoiselle is paying him; effectively he is comatose;
but that will pass. At present, I leave to make
arrangements, but will do myself the honour to
return in half an hour;" and the doctor wriggled
himself out of the house.

Morna then entered the room where the sufferer lay. The doctor had not exaggerated when
he said that there was a certain mournfulness in
the change which his patient's appearance had
undergone. It was extremely shocking and
ghastly. A deathly pallor was on his face,
which, on the left side, was somewhat distorted.
His respiration was scarcely perceptible, and the
nerveless *pose* of the unconscious figure was the
attitude of death, rather than of sleep. Marie's
little exaggeration was very pardonable. Morna
shuddered at the sight, but nerved herself, and
approached. She laid her hand on his forehead;
it was deathly cold. She raised his hand; it
too was like ice, and heavy as lead.

"He is dying!" she exclaimed; "he is certainly dying," and ran to the door. "Quick, Marie!" she exclaimed; "run for madame, and bid her hasten." Then she returned to the sufferer's side, her heart swelling with compassion.

What an end! what a death this was! So lonely—so forsaken—so desolate! If the life had been a guilty one, it had been full of sorrows; and its latest act had been one of repentance and atonement. Yet there had been no kindly words to soothe the penitent in his last hours of consciousness; no tender, loving voice to comfort and support him—to bid him be of good cheer, to tell him that he had done well at last, and that if reputation, fortune, everything else went, he had become higher, and nobler, and richer than he had ever been before. This had been denied him : he had been deserted at his utmost need; and the last day of his life had seen the severance of ties that should be the closest, and left him forlorn of the human sympathy which might have saved him.

"His last words were good," she murmured. "'The path is clear before me now. God keep me in it!'"

The doctor returned sooner than he had promised.

"Mademoiselle distresses herself unnecessarily," he said. "Undeniably the case is critical, but the symptoms are not exceptional. Skill, care, and time—*voilà tout*."

But Morna felt convinced that he was dying; and as her mother did not come, she went in quest of her.

To her surprise she found that lady sitting as she had left her, in the hotel. "Mamma!" she exclaimed, "what are you doing? why do you not come? He is dying."

"He is not dead, then, as the girl said?"

"No, no, and the doctor speaks hopefully; but there is death in his face. Come before it is too late."

"No, Morna, I have no intention of going to this man."

"What?"

"I am consistent; my conscience, the consideration of what is due to myself, my name, my origin, compelled me to fly from the contamination. Am I to go back to it, because the man is dying? His death and his life are equally nothing to me now. I don't own any connection."

" He said he was innocent, though convicted."

" They all plead 'not guilty;' but if he had been twenty times innocent, it is quite enough for me that he has dragged me down to his own degraded position, by a common swindle."

" If you saw him now you would pity him."

" All the more reason that I should *not* see him ; it would be quite immoral to pity him."

"Oh, mamma, mamma! how can you be so hard ? "

" My principles have always been strong and firm."

" This is not firmness, it is cruelty. How can you ask for forgiveness if you refuse it to others?"

" Don't preshoom to lecture me, Morna."

" You will not come, then ? "

" Certainly not."

" Then I will go to him ; he shall not be left to die alone."

" It will be just of a piece with your unruly conduct and heartlessness to me ; and very likely you will get compromised with the police by going."

But Morna was not deterred by this consideration, and she went. She was not destined, however, to perform the pious duty of closing her step-father's eyes that night. The doctor's view of the case was justified. Consciousness partially returned; the patient rallied, but his life was in the balance, and Morna remained with him.

The next day she sent a message to Eila, informing her of her father's condition ; but she and Sir Roland had left Pau that morning—for England, it was understood. She then made another attempt to induce her mother to return ; it was, however, ineffectual. Her position was a trying one; but she obeyed the dictates of her heart, and remained with the friendless man—so truly friendless that she knew not to whom she should apply; but, as a last resource, telegraphed to Mr Tainsh, as his agent, to come out.

The patient's consciousness was not fully restored for three or four days, and when it was, his speech proved to be much impaired. Nevertheless, he contrived, as he recognised Morna, and made a feeble effort to hold out his hand to her, to express his gratitude for her presence.

" You alone ; no one else ? " he asked.

" The doctor will be here soon, and your servant is in the next room."

" Eila ? "

"She has gone to England."

His grasp tightened on her hand for a moment, but he said nothing more, and, shortly
after, sank into a lethargic sleep. When he
again awoke, some hours after, he was excited
and agitated, as if by a sudden recollection.

" The papers—the papers ! " he exclaimed ;
" on the bureau, in the drawing - room ; bring
them."

The letters he had written on the night of his
seizure were found as he had left them, and
Morna laid them beside him. To see them gave
him manifest satisfaction. " Not posted," he
murmured ; " it is lucky ; " then, after looking at
them for a minute, and dreamily up into Morna's
face, as if trying to recall some lost train of
thought, "Send for a notary."

Morna despatched a messenger at once ; but
some hours elapsed before such an official could
be induced to make his appearance. In the interval Mr M'Killop again slept, and when he

awoke he was fresher and clearer than he had been before.

The notary, attended by his clerk, was shown into the sick man's room. His bureaucratic air, natural to all French officials, tempered the cosy and confidential manner due to testamentary operations.

" Monsieur could not have been more fortunate in a notary," he said ; "if an autograph is not prepared, he can dictate ; and if it deranges him to employ the French language, let him use his own. In it I declare myself to be proficient, and can draw the testament in either language."

" It is not a testament, it is a deposition," said M'Killop ; and the notary's countenance became definitely bureaucratic at once. M'Killop then made him read over the statement which he had written to Mr Tainsh, signed it, and had it duly attested by the Frenchman. He then instructed him to make a copy of it, which was also read over, signed, and duly attested. The notary insisted on making a *précis* of the statement, and, indeed, would probably have made a *précis* of the copy also, if the doctor had not arrived and summarily ejected him. The exertion and excitement had nearly prostrated the patient already, he said, and he found his situation again critical.

Three days after this Mr Tainsh arrived.

CHAPTER XL.

WE must now pass over a week or two, and rejoin Bertrand Cameron at Gosport. In the interval he had received two communications on the subject of the Aberlorna succession — one from Sir Roland, and the other that which M'Killop had written on the night he was taken ill at Pau.

To have a main object in common—viz., to inform Bertrand of the existence of the second will—two letters could not well have been more unlike, or have handled the subject in a more different manner. Sir Roland's was written as to a non-acquaintance, and contained no allusion to any other subject of mutual interest, not even to his own marriage.

"He had seen," he said, "a will purporting to be the last will of his father, and altering the disposition of the Aberlorna property so as to make

Bertrand the actual proprietor since his birth. The will was in the possession of Mr M'Killop, and had come to be so under circumstances connected with the crime for which that person had suffered punishment. His *primâ facie* view of the matter had been, that it was probably a fabrication for purposes of extortion; but he had seen the instrument, and was bound, taking a dispassionate view of the case, to admit that it bore a certain air of genuineness. Probably it was a case where a compromise might satisfy the interests of both parties, and he had instructed his agent, Mr Tainsh, in Scotland, to draw up a suitable proposal, with that view. He understood that the documents would be sent to that gentleman by Mr M'Killop, for whom he had also acted as agent; and he hoped that an arrangement might be come to, which would save the tedious, expensive, and often unsatisfactory expedient of litigation."

Mr M'Killop's version of the matter was of a very different complexion. Mr M'Killop told the truth, and the whole truth, as we know it, not excepting the part which Sir Roland had played in the attempted composition, nor this final stratagem by which he had attempted to silence M‘Killop by marrying his daughter. He went on to say that he had forwarded a full statement of the case, with the will, and every information he could give to facilitate the collection of corroborative evidence, to Mr Tainsh. That gentleman would take all necessary legal steps to replace Bertrand in his rights. He expressed his own deep contrition; explained, at length, how he had been led on, by one circumstance and another, to postpone the act he had now performed; and begged for Bertrand's forgiveness for the injury he had done him. " I do not know," he said, " in what position I shall stand with regard to the law; I fully own that I righteously deserve punishment; but, if it rests with you to bring me to it, I ask you to remember that I am an old man, and already punished bitterly by myself and by my own remorse; yet I do not ask forbearance so much on my own account, as for that of my innocent son, whose future will be ruined by my public disgrace. As far as pecuniary compensation goes for the loss you have sustained, that might be exacted by the law from Sir Roland Cameron. He, of course, will not be in a position to meet the demand, and I shall therefore offer to pay you, at once, the sum of money which was destined as my daughter's portion to come to her at my death, in the event of her marriage with yourself. As she has thought fit to become Sir Roland's wife without my consent, it seems the most natural use to which to devote the money; and I shall be prepared to make what further restitution you may require, up to my ability. I desire, in every way, to make full atonement for my offence."

To Sir Roland's letter Bertrand vouchsafed no reply.

To M'Killop he wrote in kind and generous terms; assured him of his forgiveness, and bade him set his mind at rest as to any wish or purpose on his part, to exact legal punishment. He gave him credit, he said, for the germ of honest intention which seemed to have underlain his conduct; and he made allowance for the strong temptation which had biassed his actions, unjustifiable though they were morally. "I assure you," he said, "not only of my forgiveness, but of my compassion, which I can freely accord to you now, since I can now congratulate you on having washed your hands of dishonour." As for compensation, he declined to accept a farthing.

The effect of this letter upon Mr M'Killop was that he again sent for the notary; and on this occasion that gentleman had the satisfaction of " drawing a testament."

A fortnight elapsed, but no further intelligence of the state of affairs reached Bertrand, and then, at Pigott's suggestion, he wrote to Mr Tainsh, requesting information as to the steps he was taking, and the progress of events.

Mr Tainsh had been some time at Pau when this letter was written, and, through the post, no answer came to Bertrand, and he was on the point of writing again, when the factor arrived in person at Gosport. He came direct from Pau, bringing the important documents with him, and other news besides; and the discussion and consultation which ensued, occupied a whole day, during which he and Bertrand were closeted with each other in a private room of the hotel.

It would be tedious to recount the business details of that lengthy interview. Mr Tainsh indeed made it as agreeable as he could; so much so, that any one cognisant of the question pending, might have augured from his manner that, in his opinion, Bertrand's was, beyond a doubt, the winning side. Mr Tainsh was not actually a truckling fellow, but it is a professional habit, and indeed instinct, to worship the rising sun. It will be better to let the results of the interview filter through a dialogue which took place that night, between Bertrand and Pigott, in the rooms of the latter, to which Bertrand repaired pretty late, after having dined with Mr Tainsh at the hotel, and seen him off to London by the last train.

"Holloa, Bertrand!" cried his friend, as he entered, "where have you been hiding yourself all day, and what became of you at mess-time?"

"Oh, I've had a dreadful long day of it; Mr Tainsh has been here!"

"Mr Tainsh! why didn't you produce him?"

"We were busily occupied from the moment he arrived till he started, half an hour ago.

"And I hope the result is satisfactory?"

"As far as business is concerned, entirely so; Tainsh says there is not the shadow of a doubt; it appears there was always the impression that my grandfather would make, and even that he *had* made, such a will. His own words gave that idea; and it was unlikely that a man of his family pride should permanently alienate so large a property from the main line, although he had disagreed with my father."

"And how will M‘Killop stand?"

"Ah! poor M‘Killop! Tainsh brings sad news; his part in the matter is played out. He is dead."

"Dead! Good God! how shocking! that must have been terribly sudden?"

"No, not quite sudden; it appears he had a paralytic stroke on the day he returned to Pau. On that day the whole *éclaircissement* seems to have come off, and he made his declaration in the presence of all his family, and to my—to Sir Roland Cameron, who had just announced his sudden, secret marriage to his daughter. The last announcement had greatly excited and distressed him; and I fear the unkindness of his wife and daughter had helped to bring on the attack. That same night, after all the agitation he had gone through, he wrote to me, it appears. You remember the letter I showed you?"

"Yes, and it was perfectly clear and collected."

"Well, that was the letter he wrote. He also wrote one to Mr Tainsh, with the will; and some hours after he was found by the servants lying insensible on the floor.”

“ Where was his wife ? ”

“ She had abandoned him at once on his making the confession.”

“ The female hound !   And his daughter ? ”

“ She had gone with her husband.”

“ He was left alone, then ? ”

“ Yes; but when she heard of his illness, Miss Grant came to him.”

“ And he did not die alone ? ”

“ No; he recovered from the first attack, had several interviews with Tainsh, went into the will question clearly and minutely, and made legal depositions in the case,—made a new will of his own, and, in fact, settled all his affairs, although the doctor promised him recovery.   In a fortnight after his first seizure he had another stroke, and he died of it.   Miss Grant remained with him all the time.   His wife never looked near him.”

“ Ah ! I always said Morna was the best of the lot—by a long way.   Poor old M‘Killop ! why the deuce couldn’t he have told the truth at once ?   What a lot he would have saved by it, for himself and every one else—his own life probably, too!"

"Yes; it's a miserable story, but there is one bright side to it, that he did the right thing at last. I am sincerely glad of it, not merely on selfish grounds, for he had taken measures that I should be righted, after his death, in any case. He has left fifty thousand pounds to Miss Grant."

"No!"

"He has indeed."

"Well, I will throw a stone on his cairn. I'm awfully glad."

"So am I; but probably she won't keep it."

"Not keep it?—why not?"

"I think she will probably give it to her stepsister; it would be my own feeling."

"Yes; but heaven be praised there are probably not two such idiots in the world. Oh Lord! how sick all that sort of thing makes me! No, no; Morna is too sensible,—she has a sound brain as well as a good heart."

"We'll not discuss it, then. I wish to say something to you about her, old fellow, by the by."

"It's coming," said Pigott, closing his eyes, and settling himself into an attitude of resignation.

" What is coming ? "

" Never mind ; go on."

" I have a delicacy about talking even to you, on the matter."

" Dismiss it, my dear fellow, — I'm case-hardened. I'll light a weed, though, before you begin, and put a bottle of chlorodyne beside me. There ! Now go on."

" Do you remember that fellow Duncanson who was at Cairnarvoch, last autumn ? "

" Remember him ? he will remain on my memory like a mark of the small-pox."

" Well, it seems he was the person who wrote to Sir Roland Cameron, about M‘Killop's antecedents."

" How did he know about them ? "

" Tainsh confesses that, in a fit of rage against Miss M‘Killop and everybody, he told Duncanson, and Duncanson wrote the anonymous letter. It could have been no one else, Tainsh says."

" And Duncanson's motive ? "

" Well, do you know, it seems extraordinary to me ; but Tainsh says he wanted to do me a bad turn, because he was furiously and savagely jealous of me."

" What I told you all along."

" In fact, Tainsh says that he attributed his refusal by Miss Grant——"

" She refused him ? "

" Oh yes ! "

" What merit that girl has ! "

" Tainsh says that Duncanson attributed his refusal by Miss Grant to — to — the fact that——"

" Oh, get along ! "

" Well, that she cared for me."

" Well, Duncanson was perfectly right ; at least in saying that she cared for you ; for she never could have taken a hound like him in any circumstances."

" Pigott ! "

" Any fool could have seen it ; and, what's more, Master Bertrand, you did your best—your very best—to make her care for you ; and laid her aside in a very unceremonious manner, when your venerable aunt—I beg a thousand pardons —when her step-sister came on the *tapis*."

" I meant nothing, I swear to you."

" My good man, I'm neither your director, nor

your father-confessor ; we constantly do what we don't mean."

" I ask you for your candid opinion : do you think I used her ill ? "

" Not a doubt of it."

Bertrand jumped off his chair, and began to stride about the room in his old wild way : " It's the last thing I would be guilty of to any woman ; it is unworthy of a man ; a male flirt ought to be tied up to the triangles and flogged for every offence ; and, least of all, would I willingly have caused her unhappiness, for she is the best girl I ever knew——"

" Tut, tut, man ! don't go on with all this to me ; you're playing the very devil with my new carpet ; sit down, can't you ? I don't think she bears malice. At Bournemouth, it struck me she seemed to have condoned everything."

" You don't suppose that she still cares for me, after all—all—my——"

" Say ' sad experiences.' I never asked her, you know, but I have a shrewd suspicion that, if you put the question to her, the answer would be affirmative, and perhaps another affirmative might follow another cognate question. Now, go to bed. You have over-excited me, and I shall lose half my night's rest : as Solomon says in his Song, 'I am sick of love.'"

"I like her better a thousand times now than I did then."

"Very well."

"I never dreamt of her, then."

"No, but you do now, and perhaps you wouldn't mind going and doing it in bed ; it's the proper place for the business, and my carpet is not, particularly when your dreams are somnambulistical—heavens, what a word ! Now, be off with you."

"I am certain she would make a fellow happy."

"Tell her so ; it's more than you're doing at present. Good night," and Bertrand left him.

"*Habet!*" chuckled Pigott; "I'm never wrong. Well, let it be so—he'll never do any good, until he is tied up, and he couldn't have a better keeper, perhaps; and fifty thousand pounds, too! by Jove! he'll be able to make a forest of part of the place now. It will suit me perfectly for autumn shooting. Bless them ! may they be happy !" With which benevolent feelings he turned into bed.

Mr Tainsh showed himself not only expedi-

tious, but skilful and acute, in the way he pressed
forward the will case.   He had been, as it were,
retained by M'Killop, before Sir Roland opened
the matter to him, and it may be supposed that
it was very consonant with his inclinations to
serve zealously as a lawyer upon the side of
him, who, as he shrewdly foresaw, would inevitably
become one of his principal employers.

By M'Killop's death, the criminal element was
entirely eliminated from the matter ; and a civil
action was raised for the reduction of the former
will, in favour of that now brought to light.
M'Killop's deposition was corroborated by other
evidence, direct and circumstantial ; and even by
the oral testimony of one or two rather ancient
witnesses whom Mr Tainsh had ferreted out.
The validity of the will was thus established, and
Bertrand was pronounced to be rightful owner
of Aberlorna.   It was not long in suspense,
for it was Tainsh's interest to have the matter
settled, and, being a lawyer, he knew how to
apply the screw to his fellow-craftsmen.   The
reader will perhaps be curious to know whether
Bertrand laid to heart Pigott's advice, and put the
questions to Morna which he had suggested.   It
may outrage the theories and sensibilities of some

to know the fact; but the truth must be spoken.
He did.   Perhaps that fever had blunted his
perception of the fitness of things, or perhaps
—— no matter; certain it is that he did not
retire to Aberlorna, and turn it into a wilderness,
growing a beard to his waist, shunning the face
of man, and living upon locusts and wild honey,
or their Highland equivalent.   Quite the contrary; the haste with which he made up his
mind upon Pigott's suggestion might appear to
some minds indecent; but it must be remembered
that he was a man of quick impulses.   The question was laid before Morna with very little delay;
and that clever dog, Pigott, was, as usual, right :
the answer was affirmative; and little more than
a year had elapsed from that unhappy day
on which the yacht Morna made her voyage to
Aberlorna with her cargo of cross - purposes,
before Bertrand conducted Morna back to that
paradise as its sovereign lady.   Shockingly un-
sentimental; but, if we all took to hermiting, or
dying of our first loves, earnest statesmen would
not require to cumber themselves with schemes
for the relief of posterity from the national
debt.   There was something like a lover's quarrel
between Bertrand and his bride when the settle-

ments were being arranged; the gallant bridegroom strongly insisting upon the necessity of
Morna's repudiating her step-father's bequest, in
favour of Lady Cameron. But the lady had a
will of her own, and declined to defeat the
testator's stroke of poetical justice by doing
so. As a compromise, however, she agreed to
settle half the income derived from her fortune
upon Eila; and, as Bertrand gave an equivalent sum from the rents of Aberlorna to Sir
Roland, the practical results to all parties were
the same; which is exactly how the domestic con-
stitution in man and wife ought to be worked.

Sir Roland and his wife would have been in a
bad case but for this generosity. Evil reports,
affecting the ex-governor's character, in many
respects, had followed him home from his colony.
His future employment was thereby rendered
impossible; and although the story of his complicity in a scheme to defraud his nephew did
not get wind in a definite shape, still it is not
likely that he could hope for anything of a comfortable reception if he ventured to show himself
in England. They are a good deal seen at
different Continental watering-places—apparently
on good terms; but if, as may be feared, they

have domestic differences, they must find consolation in the society of the assiduous, if not mutual, friends of the opposite sexes, who appear to rally round them with the frank devotion so characteristic of these localities. Bertrand feels his uncle's dishonour so keenly that he never even mentions the name of that recreant knight and sullier of the gallant tartan; but as long as Mr Tainsh is regular in his quarterly remittances, it is not likely that the evil old man will deeply deplore the loss of his nephew's countenance.

Mrs M'Killop's possible advent is the only other cloud that casts a shadow on the bright home at Aberlorna; hitherto it has been cast from a long distance, and those who tremble for its nearer approach can only hope that the attraction of the southern atmosphere may continue to prove as powerful as at present. "If she comes," says Pigott, who is a pretty frequent guest of his late brother officer, "leave her to me; I'll settle her." He has not divulged his proposed method of treatment, but his friends look upon him as so amazingly clever, and so perpetually in the right, that they cherish him as a sort of talisman against the threatened evil. Bertrand's private idea is, that he means to ruin her out of the place, with marked cards and cogged dice (the results to be handed over to the poor of the parish); but, if he is right, the chances are that two years spent in the society of Baron Hunkers & Co., will have taught her how to neutralise, at the least, any such stratagem. Let us hope, however, that she may come not at all, or, if at all, that she may come late and depart early.

THE END.

PRINTED BY WILLIAM BLACKWOOD AND SONS, EDINBURGH.

MESSRS BLACKWOOD & SONS'

RECENT PUBLICATIONS.

NEW WORK BY GEORGE ELIOT.

MIDDLEMARCH: A STUDY OF ENGLISH PROVINCIAL
LIFE. *[In the press.*

THE WAR FOR THE RHINE FRONTIER, 1870:
Its POLITICAL AND MILITARY HISTORY. By COLONEL W. RÜSTOW.
Translated from the German by JOHN LAYLAND NEEDHAM,
Lieutenant R.M. Artillery. In 3 vols. 8vo, with Maps and Plans,
£1, 11s. 6d. *[In the press.*

OUR POOR RELATIONS. By COL. E. B. HAMLEY, C.B.
Originally published in 'Blackwood's Magazine.' With Illustrations
from Designs by ERNEST GRISET. *[In the press.*

The THIRD VOLUME of

MEMOIRS OF THE LIFE AND TIMES OF HENRY
LORD BROUGHAM: Written by Himself. With Engraving from
the Portrait by Sir Thomas Lawrence. Complete in 3 vols. 8vo.
16s. each. *[In the press.*

LILIAS LEE AND OTHER POEMS. By JAMES BAL-
LANTINE, Author of 'The Miller of Deanhaugh;' 'The Gaber-
lunzie's Wallet.' Fcap. 8vo. *[In the press.*

ELEMENTS OF AGRICULTURAL CHEMISTRY. By
the late PROFESSOR JAMES F. W. JOHNSTON. A New Edition.
Revised and brought down to the present time by G. T. ATKINSON,
B.A. F.C.S., Clifton College. *[In the press.*

DOMESTIC VERSES.   By D. M. MOIR (Delta).   A New
Edition.   Fcap. 8vo.   *[In the press.*

AN ETYMOLOGICAL AND PRONOUNCING DIC-
TIONARY OF THE ENGLISH LANGUAGE.   FOR USE IN
SCHOOLS AND COLLEGES, AND AS A BOOK OF GENERAL REFERENCE.
In One Volume, crown 8vo.   *[In the press.*

THE COMING RACE.   Fifth Edition.   Octavo, 10s. 6d.
cloth.

" Language, literature, and the arts, all touched on with admirable
verisimilitude, are impressed into the service of his thesis; and often,
in reading of the delights of this underground Utopia, have we sighed
for the refreshing tranquillity of that lamp-lit land."—*Athenæum.*

" There is an undercurrent of humour and irony running through the
vision, it is true ; but it has, nevertheless, a half-painful, half-grotesque
air of earnestness in it, as though the writer were quite prepared to discover any day the people of which he has dreamt, and as though he
thirsted for that discovery as a solace to his soul."—*Standard.*

" The prose poem of ' The Coming Race'—for so it may justly be entitled—takes high rank among the most remarkable and original books
of the day."—*Daily Telegraph.*

A NEW SEA AND AN OLD LAND ; Being Papers
suggested by a Visit to Egypt at the end of 1869.   By W. G.
HAMLEY, Colonel in the Corps of Royal Engineers.   8vo, with
Coloured Illustrations, 10s. 6d.

MARY QUEEN OF SCOTS AND HER ACCUSERS.
By JOHN HOSACK.   A New and Enlarged Edition, continuing the
Narrative down to the Death of Queen Mary.   With a Photograph
from the Bust on the Tomb in Westminster Abbey.   In 8vo, 15s.

" He has confuted those who, by brilliant writing and a judicious selection of evidence, paint the Queen of Scots as an incarnate fiend, and who
are dramatic poets rather than historians."—*Times.*

" The story never flags, and it should be perused and reperused by every
one interested—and who is not ?—in the subject of which it treats."—
Athenæum.

" No advocate could have placed the Darnley tragedy in a better light
for Mary."—*Spectator.*

" Whatever surmises may be formed about Mary's knowledge or assent,
there can now be no doubt that the murder was contrived, not by Mary,
but by her accusers."—*Scotsman.*

Complete in Seven Volumes, 8vo, £4, 18s.

THE HISTORY OF SCOTLAND; from Agricola's Invasion to the Revolution of 1688. By JOHN HILL BURTON, Historiographer Royal.

" Mr Burton has the highest qualifications for the task. In no other history of Scotland with which we are acquainted are there the especial attractive graces which distinguish these volumes of national history."—*Athenæum.*

" But any faults—if indeed they are to be called faults—of this kind are quite overbalanced by the sterling merits of Mr Burton's book, its clearness, impartiality, and good sense. It is a business-like sort of history, which goes to the point and tells you what you really want to know."—*Saturday Review.*

" We have here a History of Scotland—*the* History of Scotland—from 84 to 1745, which will furnish Scotland with as full and faithful a record of seventeen centuries as is possessed by almost any other country in Europe."—*Scotsman.*

" Taken as a whole, we must pronounce it the most complete, and in every sense the best history of Scotland extaut."—*Examiner.*

THE METAMORPHOSES OF PUBLIUS OVIDIUS NASO. Translated in English Blank Verse by HENRY KING, M.A., Fellow of Wadham College, Oxford, and of the Inner Temple, Barrister-at-Law. Crown 8vo, 10s. 6d.

" An excellent translation."—*Athenæum.*
" The execution is admirable. . . . It is but scant and inadequate praise to say of it that it is tho best translation of the Metamorphoses which we have."—*Observer.*

THE POEMS OF OSSIAN in the Original Gaelic. With a Literal Translation into English, and a Dissertation on the Authenticity of the Poems. By the REV. ARCHIBALD CLERK. 2 vols. imperial 8vo, £1, 11s. 6d.

THE PARADISE OF BIRDS: An Old Extravaganza in a Modern Dress. By W. J. COURTHOPE, Author of 'Ludibria Lunæ.' 8vo, 5s.

THE CROWN AND ITS ADVISERS: Four Lectures on the Queen, the Ministry, the Lords, the Commons. By ALEX. C. EWALD, F.S.A., of her Majesty's Record Office. Crown 8vo, 5s.

Second Hundredth Thousand.

REMINISCENCES OF A VOLUNTEER: The BATTLE
of DORKING. From 'Blackwood's Magazine' for May. Sixpence.

THE ÆNEID OF VIRGIL. Books I.-VI. Translated
in English Blank Verse. By G. K. RICKARDS, M.A. Crown 8vo,
5s.
Preparing for Publication, completing the above,
BOOKS VII.-XII. Translated in English Blank Verse. By Lord
RAVENSWORTH.

VENUS AND PSYCHE. With other Poems. By
RICHARD CRAWLEY. Fcap. 8vo, 5s.

SONGS AND VERSES: SOCIAL AND SCIENTIFIC.
By an old Contributor to 'Maga.' A New Edition. Fcap. 8vo, 3s. 6d.
Music of some of the Songs.

"The productions thrown off by this eccentric muse have all the merits
of originality and variety. . . . He has written songs, not essays—such a
hotch-potch of science and humour, jest and literature, gossip and criti-
cism, as might have been served at the Noctes Ambrosianæ in the blue
parlour at Ambrose's."—*Saturday Review.*

ESSAYS ON SOCIAL SUBJECTS. Originally published
in the 'Saturday Review.' New Edition. 2 vols. crown 8vo, 12s.

STUDIES IN ROMAN LAW. With Comparative Views
of the Laws of France, England, and Scotland. By Lord MAC-
KENZIE, one of the Judges of the Court of Session in Scotland.
Third Edition, 8vo, 12s. 6d.

LORD ST LEONARDS' HANDY BOOK ON PRO-
PERTY LAW. A New Edition, 5s.

GRAFFITI D'ITALIA. By W. W. Story. Author of
' Robi di Roma.' In fcap. 8vo, 7s. 6d.

HOURS OF CHRISTIAN DEVOTION. Translated from
the German of Dr A. THOLUCK, by the Rev. ROBERT MENZIES,
D.D. With a Preface by the Author for this Translation. 8vo, 9s.

GOETHE'S FAUST.   Translated into English Verse by
THEODORE MARTIN. Second Edition, post 8vo, 6s. Also, An
Edition in foolscap 8vo, 3s. 6d.

"The best translation of 'Faust' in verse we have yet had in England."
—*Spectator.*

A NEW EDITION.

THE VITA NUOVA OF DANTE.   Translated, with an
Introduction and Notes, by THEODORE MARTIN. Crown 8vo, 5s.

WHAT I SAW OF THE WAR AT THE BATTLES
OF SPEICHERN, GORZE, AND GRAVELOTTE. A NARRATIVE
OF TWO MONTHS' CAMPAIGNING WITH THE PRUSSIAN ARMY OF THE
MOSELLE. By the HON. C. ALLANSON WINN. Post 8vo, with
Map, &c., 9s.

PICCADILLY: A FRAGMENT OF CONTEMPORARY BIO-
GRAPHY. By LAURENCE OLIPHANT, late M.P. for the Stirling
Burghs. With Eight Illustrations by RICHARD DOYLE. Third Edi-
tion, 6s.

"The picture of 'Good Society'—meaning thereby the society of men
and women of wealth or rank—contained in this book, constitutes its chief
merit, and is remarkable for the point and vigour of the author's style."
—*Athenæum.*

HISTORICAL SKETCHES OF THE REIGN OF GEORGE
SECOND. By MRS OLIPHANT. Second Edition, in One Volume,
10s. 6d.

"Mrs Oliphant's Historical Sketches form two attractive volumes,
whose contents are happily arranged so as to bring out some of the salient
points at a period in our social history richly illustrated by epistolary and
biographical remains."—*Examiner.*

"The most graphic and vigorous Historical Sketches which have ever
been published. It is indeed difficult to exaggerate the interest which
attaches to these two volumes, or the high literary merit by which they
are marked."—*John Bull.*

INTRODUCTORY TEXT-BOOK OF METEOROLOGY.
By ALEXANDER BUCHAN, F.R.S.E., Secretary of the Scottish
Meteorological Society; Author of 'Handy Book of Meteorology,'
&c. Crown 8vo, with 8 Coloured Charts and other Engravings, 4s. 6d.

LORD LYTTON'S NOVELS.

Library Edition. Printed from a large and readable type. In Volumes of a convenient and handsome form. 8vo, 5s. each—viz :

THE CAXTON NOVELS, 10 Volumes :

THE CAXTON FAMILY. 2 vols.
MY NOVEL. 4 vols.

WHAT WILL HE DO WITH IT ? 4 vols.

HISTORICAL ROMANCES, 11 Volumes :

DEVEREUX. 2 vols.
THE LAST DAYS OF POMPEII. 2 vols.
RIENZI. 2 vols.

THE SIEGE OF GRENADA. 1 vol.
THE LAST OF THE BARONS. 2 vols.
HAROLD. 2 vols.

ROMANCES, 7 Volumes :

THE PILGRIMS OF THE RHINE. 1 vol.
A STRANGE STORY. 2 vols.

EUGENE ARAM. 2 vols.
ZANONI. 2 vols.

NOVELS OF LIFE AND MANNERS, 15 Volumes :

PELHAM. 2 vols.
THE DISOWNED. 2 vols.
PAUL CLIFFORD. 2 vols.
GODOLPHIN. 1 vol.
ERNEST MALTRAVERS — First Part. 2 vols.

ERNEST MALTRAVERS — Second Part (*i. e.*, Alice). 2 vols.
NIGHT AND MORNING. 2 vols.
LUCRETIA. 2 vols.

GEORGE ELIOT'S WORKS :

ADAM BEDE. In crown 8vo, with Illustrations, 3s. 6d. cloth.

THE MILL ON THE FLOSS. In crown 8vo, with Illustrations, 3s. 6d. cloth.

SCENES OF CLERICAL LIFE. In crown 8vo, with Illustrations, 3s. cloth.

SILAS MARNER : The Weaver of Raveloe. In crown 8vo, with Illustrations, 2s. 6d. cloth.

FELIX HOLT, THE RADICAL. In crown 8vo, with Illustrations, 3s. 6d. cloth.

SPANISH GYPSY. Fourth Edition, crown 8vo, 7s. 6d.

WORKS OF SAMUEL WARREN, D.C.L. :

THE DIARY OF A LATE PHYSICIAN. 1 vol. crown 8vo, 5s. 6d.

Illustrated Edition, in crown 8vo, handsomely printed, 7s. 6d.

TEN THOUSAND A-YEAR. Two vols. crown 8vo, 9s.

NOW AND THEN. Crown 8vo, 2s. 6d.

MISCELLANIES. Crown 8vo, 5s.

THE LILY AND THE BEE. Crown 8vo, 2s.

WORKS OF PROFESSOR AYTOUN :

LAYS OF THE SCOTTISH CAVALIERS. An Illustrated Edition. From Designs by Sir JOSEPH NOEL PATON. Engraved by John Thompson, W. J. Linton, W. Thomas, Whymper, Cooper, Green, Dalziels, Evans, &c. In Small Quarto, printed on Toned Paper, bound in gilt cloth, 21s.

ANOTHER EDITION, the 22d, in fcap. 8vo, 7s. 6d.

BOTHWELL: A Poem. By W. EDMONDSTOUNE AYTOUN, D.C.L. Third Edition. Fcap. 8vo, 7s. 6d.

THE BALLADS OF SCOTLAND. Edited by Professor AYTOUN. Fourth Edition. 2 vols. fcap. 8vo, 12s.

POEMS AND BALLADS OF GOETHE. Translated by PROFESSOR AYTOUN and THEODORE MARTIN. Second Edition, fcap. 8vo, 6s.

THE BOOK OF BALLADS. Edited by BON GAULTIER. Eleventh Edition, with numerous Illustrations by DOYLE, LEECH, and CROWQUILL. Gilt edges, post 8vo, 8s. 6d.

FIRMILIAN ; OR, THE STUDENT OF BADAJOS. A Spasmodic Tragedy. By T. PERCY JONES. Fcap. 8vo, 5s.

MEMOIR OF WILLIAM E. AYTOUN, D.C.L., Author of

'Lays of the Scottish Cavaliers,' &c. By THEODORE MARTIN. With Portrait. Post 8vo, 12s.

SIR WILLIAM HAMILTON'S WORKS:

LECTURES ON METAPHYSICS. Edited by the Very Rev. the Dean of St Paul's, and JOHN VEITCH, M.A., Professor of Logic and Rhetoric in the University of Glasgow. Fourth Edition. 2 vols. 8vo, 24s.

LECTURES ON LOGIC. Edited by the Same. Second Edition. 2 vols. 8vo, 24s.

DISCUSSIONS ON PHILOSOPHY AND LITERATURE, EDUCATION AND UNIVERSITY REFORM. Third Edition. 8vo, 21s.

MEMOIR OF SIR WILLIAM HAMILTON, Bart.,
Professor of Logic and Metaphysics in the University of Edinburgh. By PROFESSOR VEITCH, of the University of Glasgow. 8vo, with Portrait, 18s.

LECTURES ON THE EARLY GREEK PHILOSOPHY,
AND OTHER PHILOSOPHIC REMAINS OF PROFESSOR FERRIER OF ST ANDREWS. Edited by Sir ALEX. GRANT and PROFESSOR LUSHINGTON. Two vols. post 8vo, 24s.

THE ODES, EPODES, AND SATIRES OF HORACE,
Translated into English Verse. By THEODORE MARTIN. Together with a Life of Horace. To this Edition (the Third of the Odes and Epodes) a Translation of the Satires has been for the first time added. Post 8vo, 9s.

THE ODES AND EPODES OF HORACE; A Metrical
Translation into English. With Introduction and Commentaries. By Lord LYTTON. With Latin Text. 8vo, 14s.

"We know of no book from which the English reader could gain a brighter or more living conception of the cordial heart and graceful song of the great Roman poet than from Lord Lytton's translation."—*Quarterly Review.*

THE ODYSSEY AND ILIAD OF HOMER, Translated
into English Verse in the Spenserian Stanza. By P. S. WORSLEY and PROFESSOR CONINGTON. 4 vols. crown 8vo, 39s.

SIR ARCHIBALD ALISON'S HISTORIES:

THE HISTORY OF EUROPE FROM THE COMMENCE-
MENT OF THE FRENCH REVOLUTION TO THE BATTLE
OF WATERLOO. Library Edition, 14 vols. 8vo, with Portraits and Index, £10, 10s. Cabinet Edition, 20 vols. crown
8vo, £6. People's Edition, 13 vols., £2, 11s.

ATLAS TO THE ABOVE. Containing 109 Maps and Plans
of Countries, Battles, Sieges, and Sea-Fights. In 4to. Library
Edition, £3, 3s.; People's Edition, £1, 11s. 6d.

CONTINUATION OF THE HISTORY OF EUROPE FROM
THE FALL OF NAPOLEON TO THE ACCESSION OF
LOUIS NAPOLEON. 9 vols. demy 8vo, £6, 7s. 6d. ; People's
Edition, 8 vols. crown 8vo, £1, 14s.

A NEW AND ENLARGED EDITION.

THE OPERATIONS OF WAR EXPLAINED AND
ILLUSTRATED. By EDWARD BRUCE HAMLEY, C.B., Colonel
in the Army, and Lieut.-Colonel Royal Artillery ; Commandant of the
Staff College. Second Edition, revised throughout by the Author,
and containing important additions, on the influence of Railways and
Telegraphs on War, and on the effects which the changes in Weapons
may be expected to produce in Tactics. Quarto, 17 Maps and Plans,
with other Illustrations, £1, 8s.

" The second edition of his extremely valuable treatise embraces all the
results of the most recent changes and modifications."—*Naval and Military Gazette.*

JOURNAL OF THE WATERLOO CAMPAIGN : Kept
throughout the Campaign of 1815. By GENERAL CAVALIE MER-
CER, Commanding the 9th Brigade Royal Artillery. Two vols. post
8vo, 21s.

" No actor in the terrible scene ushered in by the following day has ever
painted it in more vivid colours than the officer of artillery who led his
troops into the very heart of the carnage, and escaped to write a book
more real, more lifelike, more enthralling, than any tale of war it has ever
been our lot to read."—*Athenæum.*

ANCIENT CLASSICS FOR ENGLISH READERS.
EDITED BY
Rev. W. LUCAS COLLINS, M.A.,
Author of 'Etoniana,' 'The Public Schools,' &c.

I. HOMER: THE ILIAD. By the Editor.

"We can confidently recommend this first volume of 'Ancient Classics for English Readers' to all who have forgotten their Greek and desire to refresh their knowledge of Homer."—*Times.*

II. HOMER: THE ODYSSEY. By the Editor.

"In the 'Odyssey,' as treated by Mr Collins, we have a story-book that might charm a child or amuse and instruct the wisest man."—*Scotsman.*

III. HERODOTUS. By George C. Swayne, M.A.

"This volume altogether confirms the highest anticipations that were formed as to the workmanship and the value of the series."—*Daily Telegraph.*

IV. THE COMMENTARIES OF CÆSAR.
By ANTHONY TROLLOPE.

"The whole work is quite up to the standard of its predecessors, than saying which we can give no higher praise."—*Vanity Fair.*

V. VIRGIL. By the Editor.

"It would be difficult to describe the ' Æneid' better than it is done here, and still more difficult to find three more delightful works than the 'Iliad,' the 'Odyssey,' and the 'Virgil' of Mr Collins."—*Standard.*

VI. HORACE. By Theodore Martin.

"Though we have neither quoted it, nor made use of it, we have no hesitation in saying, that the reader who is wholly or for the most part unable to appreciate Horace untranslated, may, with the insight he gains from the lively, bright, and, for its size, exhaustive little volume to which we refer, account himself hereafter familiar with the many-sided charms of the Venusian, and able to enjoy allusions to his life and works which would otherwise have been a sealed book to him."—*Quarterly Review.*

VII. ÆSCHYLUS. By Reginald S. Copleston, M.A.
Fellow and Lecturer of St John's College, Oxford.

"The result is a really delightful little volume."—*The Examiner.*

VIII. XENOPHON. By Sir Alexander Grant, Bart.
Principal of the University of Edinburgh.

"The book is in the highest degree pleasant reading, and is certain to add to the already high and well-gained reputation of the series both among English and classical readers."—*Daily Review.*

IX. CICERO. By the Editor.

"It is almost impossible to overrate the boon conferred on the rising generation of English readers by such eminently judicious and honestly-executed treatises as this, in which Mr Collins has utilised the best lights of the modern world for the elucidation of the old."—*Courant.*

X. SOPHOCLES. By Clifton W. Collins, M.A.
H.M. Inspector of Schools.

BLACKWOOD'S
STANDARD NOVELS.

Uniform in size and legibly printed.

EACH NOVEL COMPLETE IN ONE VOLUME.

TOM CRINGLE'S LOG. By Michael Scott,	2/0
CRUISE OF THE MIDGE. By Michael Scott,	2/0
CYRIL THORNTON. By Captain Hamilton,	2/0
ANNALS OF THE PARISH. By John Galt,	2/0
THE PROVOST, AND OTHER TALES. By John Galt,	2/0
SIR ANDREW WYLIE. By John Galt,	2/0
THE ENTAIL. By John Galt,	2/0
REGINALD DALTON. By J. G. Lockhart,	2/0
PEN OWEN. By Hook,	2/0
ADAM BLAIR. By J. G. Lockhart,	2/0
LADY LEE'S WIDOWHOOD. By Colonel Hamley,	2/0
SALEM CHAPEL. By Mrs Oliphant,	2/0
THE PERPETUAL CURATE. By Mrs Oliphant,	2/0
MISS MARJORIBANKS. By Mrs Oliphant,	2/0
SIR BROOK FOSSBROOKE. By Charles Lever,	2/0
THE LIFE OF MANSIE WAUCH. By D. M. Moir,	1/0
PENINSULAR SCENES, &c. By F. Hardman,	1/0
SIR FRIZZLE PUMPKIN, NIGHTS AT MESS, &c.,	1/0
THE SUBALTERN. By G. R. Gleig,	1/0
LIFE IN THE FAR WEST. By G. F. Ruxton,	1/0
VALERIUS, A ROMAN STORY. By J. G. Lockhart,	1/0
THE RECTOR, &c. By Mrs Oliphant,	1/0

At the prices above quoted, the Volumes are in boards, with printed covers.
For 6d. extra they can be had strongly bound in cloth, lettered.

A New and Enlarged Edition of the

HANDY BOOK OF THE FLOWER-GARDEN. By
DAVID THOMSON, Gardener to the Duke of Buccleuch at Drum-
lanrig, N.B. Crown 8vo, with Engravings, 7s. 6d.

THE HANDBOOK OF HARDY HERBACEOUS
PERENNIAL AND ALPINE FLOWERS FOR THE FLOWER-
GARDEN. By WILLIAM SUTHERLAND, Gardener to the Earl
of Minto; formerly Manager of the Herbaceous Department at Kew.
In one vol. crown 8vo, 7s. 6d.

A BOOK ABOUT ROSES: How to Grow and Show
THEM. By S. REYNOLDS HOLE, Author of 'A Little Tour in
Ireland.' A New Edition, being the Third. Crown 8vo, 7s. 6d.

A PRACTICAL TREATISE ON THE CULTIVATION
OF THE GRAPE VINE. By WILLIAM THOMSON. Seventh
Edition. 8vo, 5s.

A PRACTICAL TREATISE ON THE CULTURE OF
THE PINE-APPLE. By DAVID THOMSON. 8vo, 5s.

THE BOOK OF THE GARDEN. By Charles M'Intosh.
2 vols. royal 8vo. Sold separately—viz., Architectural and Ornamental Gardening, £2, 10s.; Practical Gardening, £1, 17s. 6d.
With 1055 Engravings.

In Monthly Numbers, price 6d.

THE GARDENER; A Magazine of Horticulture and
Floriculture. Edited by DAVID THOMSON, Author of the
'Handy Book of the Flower-Garden,' 'A Practical Treatise on the
Culture of the Pine-Apple,' &c. Annual Subscription, 6s., or free by
post, 7s., payable in advance.

THE HANDY BOOK OF BEES AND THEIR PRO-
FITABLE MANAGEMENT. By A. PETTIGREW, Rusholme,
Manchester. Fcap. 8vo, with Engravings, 4s. 6d.

THE BOOK OF THE FARM, Detailing the Labours of the Farmer, Farm-Steward, Ploughman, Shepherd, Hedger, Farm-Labourer, Field-Worker, and Cattleman. By HENRY STEPHENS, F.R.S.E. Illustrated with Portraits of Animals, engraved on Steel; and 557 Engravings on Wood, representing the principal Field Operations, Implements, and Animals treated of in the Work. Third Edition, in great part Rewritten, to bring up to the present time. In Two Volumes, £2, 10s.

THE FORESTER: A Practical Treatise on the Planting, Rearing, and General Management of Forest-Trees. By JAMES BROWN, LL.D., Wood-Surveyor and Nurseryman, Stirling. Fourth Edition, brought up to the present state of the Science of Arboriculture. Royal 8vo, with Engravings, £1, 11s. 6d.

THE BOOK OF THE LANDED ESTATE; Containing Directions for the Management and Development of the Resources of Landed Property; detailing the duties of the Landlord, Factor, Tenant, Forester, and Labourer. By ROBERT E. BROWN, Factor and Estate Agent, Wass, Yorkshire. Royal 8vo, with numerous Engravings, £1, 1s.

A MANUAL OF ENGLISH PROSE LITERATURE. Designed mainly for the Assistance of Students in English Composition. By W. MINTO, M.A. [*In the press.*

ADVANCED TEXT-BOOK OF BOTANY. For the Use of Students. By ROBERT BROWN, M.A., Ph.D. Göt., F.R.G.S., Lecturer on Botany under the Science and Art Department of the Privy Council on Education. [*In the press.*

MANUAL OF ZOOLOGY. For the Use of Students. By H. ALLEYNE NICHOLSON, M.D., F.R.S.E., F.G.S., Professor of Natural History in the University of Toronto. Revised and improved Edition. Crown 8vo, 222 Engravings, 12s. 6d.
[*In the press.*

GEOGRAPHICAL WORKS

By ALEX. KEITH JOHNSTON, LL.D., F.R.S.E., F.R.G.S.

WITH THE NEW BOUNDARIES OF THE GERMAN EMPIRE,
AND OTHER RECENT INFORMATION.

I.

THE ROYAL ATLAS OF MODERN GEOGRAPHY.

A Series of entirely Original and Authentic Maps. With Indices to each
Map, comprising nearly 150,000 Names of Places contained in the Atlas.
In imperial folio, half-bound morocco, £5, 15s. 6d. Dedicated by Spe-
cial Permission to Her Majesty.

II.

THE HANDY ROYAL ATLAS.

45 Maps, clearly Printed and carefully Coloured, with General Index. In
imperial 4to, half-bound morocco, £2, 12s. 6d. Dedicated by Permission to H.R.H. the Prince of Wales.

III.

SCHOOL ATLASES.

ATLAS OF GENERAL AND DESCRIPTIVE GEOGRAPHY.
A New and Enlarged Edition, suited to the best Text-Books, with
Geographical information brought up to the time of publication.
26 Maps, clearly and uniformly printed in colours, with Index. Imperial 8vo, half-bound, 12s. 6d.

ATLAS OF PHYSICAL GEOGRAPHY. Illustrating, in a
Series of Original Designs, the Elementary Facts of GEOLOGY, HYDRO-
GRAPHY, METEOROLOGY, and NATURAL HISTORY. A New and En-
larged Edition, containing 4 new Maps and Letterpress. 20 Coloured
Maps. Imperial 8vo, half-bound, 12s. 6d.

ATLAS OF ASTRONOMY. A New and Enlarged Edition, 21
Coloured Plates. With an Elementary Survey of the Heavens, designed as an accompaniment to this Atlas, by ROBERT GRANT,
LL.D., &c., Professor of Astronomy, and Director of the Observatory
in the University of Glasgow. Imperial 8vo, half-bound, 12s. 6d.

ATLAS OF CLASSICAL GEOGRAPHY. A New and Enlarged
Edition. 23 Coloured Maps. Imperial 8vo, half-bound, 12s. 6d.

ELEMENTARY ATLAS OF GENERAL AND DESCRIP-
TIVE GEOGRAPHY, for the Use of Junior Classes; including a MAP
OF CANAAN and PALESTINE, with GENERAL INDEX. 8vo, half-bd., 5s.